U0108725

蔡英材　編著

速決英語難點

HIT THE MARK :
A QUICK-AND-EASY
ENGLISH GUIDE

商務印書館

速決英語難點 *Hit the Mark : A Quick-and-Easy English Guide*

作　　者：蔡英材

責任編輯：黃家麗

封面設計：張　　毅

出　　版：商務印書館 (香港) 有限公司

香港筲箕灣耀興道 3 號東滙廣場 8 樓

http://www.commercialpress.com.hk

發　　行：香港聯合書刊物流有限公司

香港新界大埔汀麗路 36 號中華商務印刷大廈 3 字樓

印　　刷：陽光印刷製本廠有限公司

香港柴灣安業街 3 號新藝工業大廈 (6 字) 樓 G 及 H 座

版　　次：2014 年 6 月第 1 版第 1 次印刷

© 2014 商務印書館 (香港) 有限公司

ISBN 978 962 07 1926 4

Printed in Hong Kong

版權所有　不得翻印

Introduction
自 序

　　各位讀者，很高興能透過文字與大家見面，我很感謝大家購買本書。這是我 1997 年從澳洲回港後，開始撰寫的第 11 本英語學習書。本書旨在幫助讀者用適當方法學英文，內容分五大類，包括：常犯英文錯誤、常用句式、常見慣用語、實用詞彙及詞組、常用詞類等，其中以避免錯誤至為重要。目前一般人最弱的是語法，很多人寫作時，往往因為語法錯誤太多，以至別人根本無法理解文章內容。

　　多年來我一直強調的原則是“簡單英文就是好英文”(Simple English is good English.)。簡單英文指符合基本語法規則的英文句子。可惜，很多人語法不夠好，也不願意下苦功學習。我始終認為，語法不好很難寫出簡單易明的文章，打好語法基礎之後，寫作時如能善用書內所教的常用句式、實用詞彙、慣用語等，行文將更流暢，加上平時多接觸英文，多下苦功，就可以提升英文水平。

　　筆者本着濃厚的熱誠和興趣從事英語教學，惟水平有限，書中錯漏難免，希望各方有識之士指正。

How to write better English
英文怎樣寫得更好

　　首先，文章基本上由幾段文字組成，而一段的字數有多少視乎全篇文章的字數而定。例如，我們需要寫 300 字的文章，除了第一段的引言 (Introduction) 和最後一段的結論 (Conclusion) 之外，一般可以寫三四段說明三四個要點。因此，一段的字數大約是 60 至 80 字。通常在每段的開始或結尾寫主題句 (Topic sentence)，然後在每段內圍繞着這個主題句加入約 30 至 40 字的解釋 (Explanation) 和例子 (Example)。由於在公開考試中，時間控制非常重要，大家必須留意每段的字數，以免到最後可能只寫得一兩段，導致嚴重失分。這些基本寫作技巧相信大家都懂，但大家感到頭痛的是怎樣寫出一句句完成段落發展 (Paragraph development) 呢？

　　事實上，大家覺得英文作文很難，主要因為不熟悉語法規則，不知道怎樣遣詞造句，引起許多語法錯誤。例如句子第一個字是名詞，名詞有多少類，名詞後跟動詞，動詞有多少類，可以如何使用，然後動詞後跟甚麼？如此類推，相信大家會"腦爆"，覺得太麻煩，不想寫了。因此，很多同學習慣按中文意思譯為英文，但問題是翻譯不容易學。詞彙的普通翻譯不難，但若大家用過機器和電腦進行句子翻譯，就知道那些翻譯有多棒！不過，若不用中文翻譯，大家一定會說不知道怎樣開始寫。

　　正如我在自序裏說，本書的目的是幫助大家改善英語尤其是寫作方面的水平。要學好英文寫作大家必須按照這書的五大範疇學習。當然大家會問為甚麼要集中於語法要點、常用句式、實用詞彙、常見慣用語和常用詞類呢？

英文語法不好寫不了好文章，相信我不用再說了。基本上，大家現時在公開考試的英文作文分數很低或甚至不合格，主要由於語法錯誤太多。目前情況是，文章如沒有語法錯誤，那篇文章已非常不錯。

其實在五六十年代，要學好英語，除了打好語法基礎外，還需要閱讀各類文章，把實用和優美的詞彙和用語抄在筆記簿上，然後經常溫習，記住它們，在適當時候應用出來。我明白大家現時閱讀文章的時間實在不多，故我在本書介紹常用句式、實用詞彙、慣用語，以幫助大家完成句子。在寫作時，只要在每段應用已學會的句式、詞彙和慣用語，自然很容易可以寫完一段。學好上述五個範疇之後，就會充滿信心，以後不再怕英文作文。

Contents
目錄

II　Common sentence patterns　常用句式

III　Idioms commonly used　常見慣用語

IV Useful vocabulary and expressions 實用詞彙及詞組

V Words of high frequency   常用詞類

注：本書用 * 標示含錯誤的句子

1 according to 不後接 opinion

我們常説 "根據 / 從……來看" 英語是 according to，表示消息源自別人或其他地方，而非自已。例如：

> According to these figures, his company is doing well.
>
> 從這些數字來看，他公司經營得不錯。

它還可暗示我們不同意別人的觀點。例如：

> According to Peter, I owed him $1,000.
>
> 根據彼得的説法，我欠他一千元。

但我們不應把 according to 與 opinion、view 等詞連用。例如："按資方的説法" 可以是 According to the management, ... 或 In the management's opinion / view, ... 。

我們不可説 According to *the management's opinion / view, ... 。更不應説 According to *me, ... ，應説 In my opinion, ... 。

Compare patterns

> According to Susan, they are not coming.
>
> 蘇珊説他們不來了。

> Who, in your opinion, is the best student in the class?
>
> 你認為哪個是班上的最佳學生？

Try the test

☐ 1. According to Peter, you owe us $1,000.

☐ 2. According to Peter's opinion, you have done a good job.

1. ✓ 2. ✗

2   in accordance with 與 according to 不可替換使用

according to 表示 "根據別人的看法或其他消息來源。" in accordance with 也有 "根據" 的意思，但它接近 "按照、依據和依照規則／法律／意願，與……一致" 的意思。例如：

In accordance with her wishes, she was buried in Guangzhou.
按她的遺願，她給安葬在廣州。

In accordance with your order, I cancelled the meeting.
按你的命令，我取消了這次會議。

He must be treated in accordance with the rules of international convention.
必須按國際公約的規則待他。

Compare patterns

The bank then invests the money in accordance with state law.
銀行然後按州法律投資那筆錢。

According to police, Peter was arrested at the scene of the robbery.
根據警方的說法，彼得於搶劫案當場被捕。

Try the test

☐   1. Susan stayed in the hotel in accordance with Peter.

☐   2. Susan stayed in the hotel, according to the manager.

1. ✗   2. ✓

3　車在路上發生故障，英文該怎説？

break down 是 "機器發生故障、汽車拋錨" 的意思。例如：

The photocopiers <u>are</u> always <u>breaking down</u>.

影印機老是發生故障。

The car <u>broke down</u> just south of Tsuen Wan.

汽車就在荃灣以南地方拋錨了。

break 的本義是 "打破、破碎、折斷" 的意思。例如：

He had to <u>break</u> the window to get into the house.

他要打破一扇窗才進到屋子裏。

She kept pulling at the rope until it <u>broke</u>.

她拉呀拉直到拉斷繩子。

He fell downstairs and <u>broke</u> his hip.

他從樓梯上摔下來，髖部骨折。

break 也有 "弄壞、損壞" 的意思。例如：

Someone <u>has broken</u> the TV.

有人弄壞了電視機。

The washing machine <u>has broken</u> again.

洗衣機又壞了。

Compare patterns

The machine <u>has broken down</u>.

那機器發生了故障。

Old bones <u>break</u> easily.

老骨頭容易折斷。

Try the test

☐　1. Our car was broken down and we had to push it off the road.

☐　2. She fell and broke her arm.

1. ✗　2. ✓

4   by all means 若沒有 -s 就出問題

有些名詞本身帶 -s，-s 屬於不可缺的一部分。例如：means 是 "方式、方法、途徑"。以下是常與 means 搭配的形容詞：

A	cost-effective	means
	chief	
	powerful	
	reliable	
	dominant	
	primary	

含 means 的常用語還有 a means of transport "交通工具"，a means to an end "達到目的的途徑／手段"。

此外，by all means 是 "可以、當然行、沒問題"，to live within your means 是 "量入為出"。

最常見的語法規則，是可數名詞若多於一個，會加 -s 表示複數。例如：boys, books, tables, cars 等。不可數名詞因為抽象或沒有實體，故不加 -s。例如：advice, traffic, equipment, information 和 luggage。

還有一些不可數名詞加 -s 之後意思會不同，例如：paper 解作 "紙張" 時是不可數名詞，不可加 -s。但加 -s 後則解作 "報紙、論文"。

Compare patterns

We need to find some other means of transportation.

我們需要找到一些其他交通工具。

Can you give me some advice?

你給我一些意見好嗎？

Try the test

☐   1. Where is my lugguage?

☐   2. Where are my lugguages?

1. ✓   2. ✗

5 別混淆 come 和 go

很多人會混淆 come 和 go，如果說某人向着或跟隨說話人來，說話人大多是他或她公司的同事。例如：

She <u>comes</u> to work by bus.
她乘公共汽車上班。

如果說某人離開說話人去上班的地方，說話人可能是家人。例如：

She <u>goes</u> to work by bus.
她乘公共汽車上班。

He <u>is coming</u> home soon.
他快回家了。

如果說話人是他公司的同事，可以說：

He <u>is going</u> home soon.
他快要（離開公司）回家了。

They'<u>ll come</u> to stay for a week.
他們要來（說話人那裏）逗留一星期。

若指某人要離開說話人去其他地方逗留一個星期，可以說：

She'<u>ll go</u> to stay for a week.
她去逗留一星期。

Compare patterns

I <u>went</u> to Japan last month.
上個月我去了日本。

There <u>is</u> a car <u>coming</u>!
一輛汽車正駛過來！

Try the test

☐ 1. Can you come to my party?

☐ 2. Can you go to my party?

1. ✓ 2. ✗

6　*You are easy to fall down. 這句錯在哪裏？

要表達 "你很易跌倒。"，不是 *You are easy to fall down.，應是 You will fall down <u>easily</u>.。又如表達 "木屋很易着火"，應是 Wooden huts catch fire <u>easily</u>. 不是 Wooden huts are <u>easy</u> to catch fire.。

記着以下原則，可減少出錯機會：

John is <u>easy</u> to please. = To please John is <u>easy</u>.

The book is <u>easy</u> to read. = To read the book is <u>easy</u>.

Easy 是形容詞和副詞，Easily 是副詞，兩者用法不同。例如：

The washing machine is <u>easy</u> to install.

那洗衣機容易安裝。

It is <u>easy</u> to see why she is so popular.

不難看出她為何那樣受歡迎。

I can <u>easily</u> finish it today.

我今天可毫不費力完成它。

He gets bored <u>easily</u>.

他容易生厭。

Compare patterns

Ever since the illness, I get tired very <u>easily</u>.

自從生了那場病，我很容易感到累。

It is <u>easy</u> to see why he is so popular.

不難看出他為何那麼受歡迎。

Try the test

☐　1.　I can easy be home, if you want.

☐　2.　I can easily be home, if you want.

1. ✗　　2. ✓

7　even 不是連詞，別將它和 even if 混淆

中文常說 "即使、甚至、連……"，英文用 even 來表達這個意思，請注意不要將它和 even if 混淆。

首先，even 是副詞，強調 "出乎意料"。例如：

He never <u>even</u> opened the box.

他根本沒打開過那個箱。

It was hot there <u>even</u> in winter.

那裏即使冬天也很熱。

<u>Even</u> a child can do it.

連小孩也能做到。

但 even 不是連詞，不像 even if / even though 可以連接從句 (subordinate clause)。even if / even though 有 "縱然、雖然" 的意思。例如：

I hope I can come back, <u>even if</u> it is only for a few weeks.

雖然只是幾個星期，我都希望可以回來。

<u>Even though</u> it was raining, we had to go out.

即使下雨，我們還是要外出。

Compare patterns

<u>Even</u> a child can understand it.

連小孩也能明白它。

<u>Even if</u> it rains, I will go.

即使下雨我也去。

Try the test

☐　1.　You haven't even finished your lunch.

☐　2.　Even you have finished your lunch, we are not going.

1. ✓　2. ✗

8　everyday 要後接名詞

很多人經常混淆 every day 和 everyday，以為兩者都是一樣。請注意，every day 是 "每天"，如表示 "天天免費泊車"，用 free parking every day。everyday "不是每天"，是形容詞，解作 "日常" 的意思，everyday objects 則是 "日常物品"。例如：

> The internet has become part of <u>everyday</u> life.
> 互聯網已成為日常生活的一部分。

> It is a small dictionary for <u>everyday</u> use.
> 它是一本常用小詞典。

如果大家還是分不開兩者，可以這樣記住："每年" 是 every year，沒有 *everyyear。所以 "每晚" 是 every night；"每星期" 是 every week。"每月" 是 every month，都是兩個字分開。因此，"每天" 是 every day，不是 everyday。請記着：everyday 的後面是有名詞的！

某大地產集團的海報說 *free parking everyday 是不對的！應是 Free parking <u>every day</u>。

Compare patterns

> We were made to attend meetings <u>every day</u>.
> 我們要每天開會。

> The book is written in simple <u>everyday</u> language.
> 那本書用簡單日常語寫成。

Try the test

☐　1.　She swims everyday.

☐　2.　We are open every day except Sunday.

1. ✗　　2. ✓

9 別混淆 firstly 與 at first

firstly 是第一，也作 first。

firstly 和 first (of all) 可引出一系列的事實、理由或意見。例如：

> Our brochure is divided into two sections, dealing firstly with basic courses and secondly with advanced ones.
>
> 我們的小冊子分兩部分：第一部分涉及基礎課程，第二部分涉及高級課程。

> There are two good reasons why we can't do it. Firstly, we don't have enough money, and secondly, we don't have enough time.
>
> 我們有兩個合理原因不做這事：第一，我們資金不足，第二，我們時間不夠。

at first 講述最初階段，尤其指與後來不同的情況作出比較。例如：

> Peter had seen her nearly every day at first. Now he saw her much less.
>
> 彼得起初幾乎每天都見她，現在見她的次數少了很多。

Compare patterns

Firstly, we don't have enough money.

第一，我們不夠錢。

Peter had seen her nearly every day at first.

起初，彼得幾乎每天都見她。

Try the test

☐   1. Firstly, we don't have enough money.

☐   2. Peter had seen her nearly every day firstly.

1. ✓   2. ✗

10   *get on the car / taxi 錯在哪裏？

很多人説 *Get on the car / taxi.，這是不對的。

在某齣鐵金剛電影，男女主角經常開車接載對方，請人上車時是 get in 而不是 get on。

記着，我們從小學會的 get on / off 是乘坐公共交通工具，例如火車、電車、巴士、輪船和飛機，因為它們是大型交通工具，所以我們是 "上落" get on / off the train / tram / bus / ferry / plane.。

但必須留意的是，乘坐計程車和私家車時，需要彎身鑽入車廂，所以是 get in the car.。從車廂裏鑽出來時，那是 get out of the car.。同樣，我們 get in / out of the boat.。

如果我們説 get on the car / boat.，人家會爬上車子 / 小船的頂部坐下來。

Compare patterns

I think we got on the wrong bus.

我想我們上錯了公共汽車。

He got in the taxi.

他上了那部計程車。

Try the test

☐   1. She got out of the car.

☐   2. She got off the car.

1. ✓   2. ✗

11　別混淆 hard 和 hardly

我們學完 hard 之後，必須留意它與 hardly 無關。hardly 是副詞，意思是 "幾乎不、幾乎沒有、很少"。例如：

I <u>hardly</u> ever go to concerts.

我很少去聽音樂會。

I can <u>hardly</u> believe it.

我幾乎不敢相信。

I can <u>hardly</u> wait for my birthday.

我急切等待着我的生日。

We <u>hardly</u> know each other.

我們彼此不太認識。

There is <u>hardly</u> any tea left.

沒剩下甚麼茶了。

這個詞不能代替 hard，所以，"今天我一直努力工作。" 不是 *I've been working hardly today.，而是 I've been working <u>hard</u> today.。"外面雨下得很大。" 不是 *It was raining hardly outside.，是 It was raining <u>hard</u> outside.。

Compare patterns

I can <u>hardly</u> wait for the news.

我急不及待想聽到這個消息。

I tried so <u>hard</u> to please him.

我盡了很大努力去取悅他。

Try the test

☐　1. The snow has frozen hardly.

☐　2. The snow has frozen hard.

1. ✗　2. ✓

12 比較英美英語：Have you got... / Do you have...?

在英式英語，have got 常用於現在式的肯定句、否定句和疑問句。例如：

They <u>have got</u> a wonderful house.
他們有一棟漂亮房子。

We <u>haven't got</u> a television.
我們沒有電視機。

<u>Have you got</u> a meeting today?
你今天要開會嗎？

以 do 構成疑問句和否定句也常見。例如：

<u>Do</u> you have any brothers?
你有兄弟嗎？

We <u>don't</u> have a car.
我們沒有汽車。

美式英語通常用 have 及 have 和 do / does / did 表示。例如：

They <u>have</u> a wonderful house.

We <u>don't have</u> a television.

<u>Do</u> you <u>have</u> a meeting today?

> Note：表示習慣或常規時，英式和美式英語都用以下說法：
> We don't often <u>have</u> time to exercise.
> 我們沒時間經常做運動。

Compare patterns

We <u>haven't got</u> a television.
我們沒有電視機。

<u>Do</u> you <u>have</u> any brothers?
你有沒有兄弟？

Try the test

- ☐　1.　We don't have got a car.
- ☐　2.　Do you a meeting today?
- ☐　3.　We haven't got a television.

1. ✗　　2. ✗　　3. ✓

13　似同非同：**hear** 和 **listen to**

hear 常表示某種聲音進入我們耳朵，即是我們自自然然地聽到的聲音。例如：

> Suddenly I <u>heard</u> a strange noise.
> 我突然聽到一種奇怪的聲音。

listen to 表示注意正在持續發出的聲音，強調集中注意力，想盡量聽清楚。你即使不聽也能 hear 某種聲音，但你只能有意識地 listen to 某種聲音。例如：

> I <u>didn't hear</u> the phone because I <u>was listening to</u> the radio.
> 我沒聽見電話響，因我在聽收音機。

> Note：hear 通常不用於進行式。要講說話時聽到甚麼，常用 can hear，特別是在英式英語。例如：
> I can <u>hear</u> somebody coming.
> 我聽見有人來了。

若要問別人 " 你在聽嗎？" 是 <u>Are</u> you <u>listening</u>?，而不是 *<u>Are</u> you <u>hearing</u>?

Compare patterns

I <u>am listening</u> to music.

我在聽音樂。

I <u>heard</u> him say so.

我聽見他這樣說。

Try the test

☐   1. I can't hear very well.

☐   2. She never hears my advice.

1. ✓   2. ✗

14 別混淆 high 和 tall

high 指"從底到頂的高度"。例如：

> The wall is over 60 feet high.
>
> 這圍牆有 60 多呎高。

> They have climbed some of the world's highest mountains.
>
> 他們攀登過幾座世界最高峰。

high 也可表示"離地面的距離"。例如：

> How high was the plane when the engine failed?
>
> 發動機發生故障時飛機離地面多高？

當我們指人時，會用 tall。例如：

> My sister is much taller than me.
>
> 我姐姐比我高多了。

但是說"他六呎高。"是 He is six feet tall. 不是 *He is six feet high.。

如果物件又高又窄，我們可以用 tall。例如：

> She broke a tall glass.
>
> 她打破了一隻高身玻璃杯。

Compare patterns

> He is much taller than me.
>
> 他比我高得多。

> The ceilings are very high.
>
> 天花板很高。

Try the test

☐ 1. She is five feet high.

☐ 2. The building is not very tall.

1. ✗   2. ✓

15   hundred, thousand, dozen 等，後加 -s 含意不同

對於 hundred, thousand, million, billion 和 dozen，許多人總是忘記，它們前面若有數字，詞尾就不加 -s，也不連接 of。在 several 和 a few 後面也是這樣。例如：

> I have three hundred dollars.
> 我有三百元。

> The company employs five thousand people.
> 公司僱用着五千名員工。

說 "我想買兩打蛋。"，是 I want to buy two dozen eggs.，不是 *I want to buy two dozens eggs.，更不是 *I want to buy two dozens of eggs.。

說 "這本書出售了三百多萬冊"，是 The book sold more than three million copies.。

但它們前面若沒有數字，後面又有 of，即 "數以……計、很多" 的意思，詞尾就必須有 -s。例如：

> Dozens of people were killed in the earthquake.
> 好幾十人在地震中喪生。

> She has had hundreds of boy friends.
> 她有很多男朋友。

Compare patterns

> Please give me two hundred dollars.
> 請給我兩百元。

> I have spoken to him dozens of time.
> 我已跟他說過很多次。

Try the test

☐   1. Please give me half a dozen of eggs.

☐   2. I want half a dozen eggs.

1. ✗   2. ✓

16   比較英美英語：ill

在英式英語中，ill 常表示"身體不適"。在美式英語中，ill 除了用於正式文體外，是不常用的。

ill 最常用於動詞後面。例如：

> Peter didn't come in last week because he was ill.
>
> 彼得上星期沒來，因為他病了。

若用於名詞前面，英國人喜歡用 sick。 美國人在非正式場合也用 sick 表示"身體不適"。例如：

> She spent twenty years looking after her sick mother.
>
> 她花了二十年照顧生病的母親。

> Note：sick 可以指"嘔吐"。例如：
> She was sick three times in the night.
> 她夜裏嘔吐了三次。
> I feel sick. Where is the toilet?
> 我覺得噁心，廁所在哪裏？

Compare patterns

> I felt ill so I went home.
>
> 我感到不適，所以回家。

> Peter reported sick.
>
> 彼得告病假。

Try the test

☐   1. The President is a very ill man.

☐   2. I am visiting my sick uncle in hospital.

1. ✗   2. ✓

17　記住 in time 與 on time 的區別

in time 是 "及時、來得及" 的意思。例如：

> Will you be <u>in time</u> for the 9 o'clock train?
>
> 你來得及趕上九點鐘那班火車嗎？

> The ambulance got there just <u>in time</u>.
>
> 救護車正好及時趕到那裏。

on time 是 "準時" 的意思。例如：

> The plane arrived <u>on time</u>.
>
> 這班飛機準時到達。

> Why is that the trains never run <u>on time</u>?
>
> 為甚麼火車從不準時到達？

總之， in time 是"在預定時間之前"；on time 就是"剛好在預定的時間"。我們想記住它們有兩個方法："in、on；及、準"；或 "in 及；on 準"。

Compare patterns

> The train arrived <u>on time</u>.
>
> 火車準時到達。

> Will we be <u>in time</u> for the 5 o'clock plane?
>
> 我們能及時趕到五點鐘的飛機嗎？

Try the test

☐　1. The ambulance came just on time.

☐　2. They got there just in time.

1. ✗　　2. ✓

18   比較 little 和 a little；a little 和 a few

a little 是一些，little 是不多。其實，兩者之間的區別與 few 和 a few 的區別一樣。只是 little / a little 與單數名詞連用，而 few / a few 與複數詞連用。

a little / a few 是"一點、一些、幾個" 的意思，與 some 意思接近。例如：

> Would you like a little soup?
>
> 你想要一點湯嗎？

> We have a few tomatoes and some pork.
>
> 我們有幾個番茄和一些豬肉。

little / few 是 "很少、不多、沒多少" 的意思。相當於 not much / not many，常有否定意思。例如：

> The average councillor has little real power.
>
> 普通議員沒多少實權。

> Few people can speak a foreign language perfectly.
>
> 很少人能説得一口很地道的外語。

Compare patterns

> I have read only a little of the report so far.
>
> 這報告我才讀了一小部分。

> She said little or nothing about her past.
>
> 她對自己的過去幾乎隻字不提。

Try the test

☐   1. Her English is improving little by little.

☐   2. Please give me little milk.

1. ✓   2. ✗

19　比較英美英語：mad 和 crazy

在美國，mad 是指 "很生氣、氣憤"。

mad 是非正式用語，用作英式英語時，表示 "瘋顛、神經錯亂、有精神病" 的意思。例如：

He thought he would go <u>mad</u> if he stayed any longer.

他想如再多留一會，他就會發瘋。

They realized that he had gone <u>mad</u>.

他們意識到他瘋了。

I will go <u>mad</u> if I have to wait much longer.

如果還要再等更長時間，我會發瘋的。

> Note：在美式英語裏，不常用 mad 表達以上意思，而用 crazy。例如：
>
> A <u>crazy</u> old woman rented the upstairs room.
> 一個瘋老太婆租了樓上那間房。
>
> 在美式英語裏，mad 是 "很生氣、氣憤" 的意思。例如：
>
> He is <u>mad</u> at me for being late.
> 我遲到了，他非常氣憤。

Compare patterns

He must be <u>crazy</u> to lend her money.

他借錢給她，一定是瘋了。

I will go <u>mad</u> if I wait much longer.

如果還要再等更長時間，我會發瘋的。

Try the test

☐　1.　What a mad idea?

☐　2.　That noise is driving me crazy.

1. ✗　2. ✓

20 "經常"是 often 不是 always

always 是 at all times.

許多人不知道"經常、時常和常常"是 often 不是 always。

記着 always 是"總是、老是、一直、永遠、每次都"的意思。英語是 at all times。

粵語的"成日"可能是 always，也可能是 often。這需由全句意思來決定。例如：

> He is always telling lies.
>
> 他成日講大話。
>
> She always gets up at 7 a.m. every day.
>
> 她總是天天早上七時便起牀。

Note：説"他整天總是看電視。"，不是 *He always watches television. 而是 He often watches television.，因他沒可能在沒特定情況下不停看電視。

同樣，説"我不經常吃餃子。"不是 *I don't always eat dumplings.，而是 I don't often eat dumplings.。

Compare patterns

> Always lock your car.
>
> 每次都要鎖車。
>
> How often do you go to the theatre?
>
> 你多久看一次戲？

Try the test

☐ 1. I see her quite always.

☐ 2. Try to exercise as often as possible.

1. ✗   2. ✓

21 open 是動詞也是形容詞

我們知道 open 是 "打開、開啟" 的意思，它是動詞。例如：

Mr. Wong <u>opened</u> the car door for his wife.

黃先生為太太打開車門。

Shall I <u>open</u> another bottle?

要不要我再開一瓶？

She <u>opened</u> the letter and read it.

她拆開信讀起來。

> Note：它也是形容詞，它是 "開着、敞開、開放" 的意思。例如：
> A fly flew in the <u>open</u> window.
> 一隻蒼蠅從打開的窗飛進來。
> She had left the door wide <u>open</u>.
> 她把房門敞開着。
> The new store will be <u>open</u> soon.
> 新店快將開業。

說 *The library is opened from 10 a.m. to 8 p.m. daily 是錯的，因這句的 open 是 "開放"，不是 "打開"，應改為 The library is <u>open</u> from 10 a.m. to 8 p.m. daily。它的反義詞是 closed.

Compare patterns

Please <u>open</u> the door for me.

請為我開門。

He left the door wide <u>open</u>.

他讓門開着。

Try the test

☐   1. The window is open.

☐   2. She had difficulty keeping her eyes opened.

1. ✓   2. ✗

22   比較 person 和 people

對於英語名詞，最重要明白它有單數和複數。最簡單的規則，是在一個普通名詞的字尾加 -s 表示複數。例如 boy, girl, toy 的複數是 boys, girls, toys。但必須留意一些常用的特別詞語不可出錯。例如 person 是"人"的意思，它是單數，它的複數形式是 people，但在正式文章卻是 persons。例如：

She is just the person we need for the job.

她正是我們所需的合適人選。

At least eight people were killed in the accident.

至少八個人在意外中喪生。

> Note：peoples 是 "各民族的人"。

Compare patterns

There were a lot of people at the party.

聚會上有很多人。

What is he like as a person?

他人品怎樣？

Try the test

☐   1. I am really not a city people.

☐   2. The price is $100 per person.

1. ✗   2. ✓

23 "玩樂器和做運動"用 play

play 是"玩耍、遊戲、玩樂"的意思。例如：

A group of kids <u>were playing</u> with a ball.

一群孩子在街上玩球。

We will have to <u>play</u> inside today.

我們今天只能在屋裏玩耍。

Let's <u>play</u> another game.

咱們玩點別的遊戲吧。

> Note：要表達"沒有人跟我玩。"，不是 *I haven't got anybody to <u>play</u>.，而是 I haven't got anybody to <u>play</u> with.。

另外，play the piano / violin / flute 等是"彈撥、吹奏(樂器)、演奏鋼琴、小提琴、笛子"的意思，不是 *play piano / violin / flute。

但 play football / basketball / tennis / golf 是"踢足球 / 打籃球 / 打排球 / 打高爾夫球"。

慣用語 There's a time to work and a time to <u>play</u>. 是"工作有時，玩樂有時。"的意思。

He <u>played</u> dead. 是"他裝死。"的意思。

Compare patterns

They <u>were playing</u> in the garden.

他們在花園玩耍。

She <u>is playing</u> the violin.

她在拉小提琴。

Try the test

☐ 1. He likes playing guitar.

☐ 2. They were playing basketball in the park.

1. ×　　2. ✓

24 prepare 和 prepare for 不能互換

prepare 是 "準備、預備、做、繪製" 的意思。例如：

I <u>was preparing to</u> leave.

我正準備離開。

He <u>was preparing</u> a report.

他正在準備一份報告。

She <u>was</u> in the kitchen <u>preparing</u> dinner.

她在廚房預備晚飯。

Who <u>prepared</u> these building plans?

這些建築圖樣是誰繪製的？

prepare for 解作 "有心理準備"，並非 "真正着手做"。例如：

<u>Prepare</u> yourself <u>for</u> a shock.

有件事會令你大吃一驚，你要做好思想準備。

The whole class is working hard <u>preparing for</u> the exams.

全班都正在努力準備考試。

Compare patterns

Please <u>prepare</u> a report <u>for</u> me.

請給我擬定報告。

I <u>was not prepared for</u> all problems.

我對所有問題毫無準備。

Try the test

☐ 1. We are not prepared to accept these conditions.

☐ 2. She was preparing for dinner in the kitchen.

1. ✓   2. ✗

25   似同非同：**purpose** 和 **aim**

aim 是要某人某事的目的。

purpose 和 aim 都是 "目的、目標" 的意思。例如：

> Our campaign's main <u>purpose</u> is to raise money.
>
> 我們這次活動，主要目的是籌款。

> What was the <u>purpose</u> of his visit?
>
> 他到訪的目的是甚麼？

> He went to Japan with the <u>aim</u> of finding a job.
>
> 他去日本是為了找工作。

> Our main <u>aim</u> is to increase sales in China.
>
> 我們主要的目標，是增加在中國的銷售量。

> Note：purpose 指做某事的原因；aim 則指要達到目的。aim 可指嘗試達到目的；purpose 含要成就某事的強烈感覺。aim 可指某人的目的，也可指某事的目的。purpose 也常指做某事的原因，也可指某人的目的，這樣屬於比較正式的用法。

Compare patterns

> What was the <u>purpose</u> of his visit?
>
> 他到訪的目的是甚麼？

> Our main <u>aim</u> is to increase sales in China.
>
> 我們主要的目標，是增加在中國的銷售量。

Try the test

☐   1. What was the purpose of his visit?

☐   2. He went to Japan with the purpose of finding a job.

1. ✓   2. ✗

26　quick 與 fast 有時不能互換

quick 是 "快、迅速、時間短暫" 的意思，通常是形容詞。例如：

These cakes are very <u>quick</u> and easy to make.

這些蛋糕做起來又快又容易。

Are you sure this is the <u>quickest</u> way?

你肯定這是最快的方法嗎？

quickly 是它的副詞，例如：

I <u>quickly</u> realized that I was on the wrong bus.

我很快意識到坐錯了公共汽車。

fast 是 "快、迅速、敏捷" 的意思，它是形容詞，也是副詞。例如：

Who is the <u>fastest</u> runner?

誰是世界最快的跑手？

> Note： fast 指 "某人或某物移動的速度"。例如：Can't you drive any <u>faster</u>? 是 "你難道不能開快一點？"，但不說 *You're driving too quickly，更沒有 *fastly。

Compare patterns

It is a <u>fast</u> car.

這車速度很快。

The kids are <u>quick</u> to learn.

這些孩子學得很快。

Try the test

☐　1. His fast thinking saved her life.

☐　2. I do not like fast food.

1. ✗   2. ✓

27 比較 shop 和 store

在英式英語中，shop 常表示"商店"的意思。例如：

> There is a book / clothes / record / sweet <u>shop</u> at the corner of the street.
>
> 街角有一間書 / 服裝 / 唱片 / 糖果店。

a barber's / betting shop 是"理髮 / 投注店"。例如：

> He went to the <u>shop</u> to buy some cookies.
>
> 他去商店買一些曲奇餅乾。

在美式英語中，store 只表示很大的 shop。在 store 裏可買到許多不同種類的東西。香港某超級市場就有 mega store。例如：

> Harrods is a famous department <u>store</u>.
>
> 哈羅茲是一家著名的百貨公司。

a DIY / furniture store 是 "DIY / 傢具商場"，a liquor store 是 "賣酒的商店"，a convenience store 是 "便利店"。

Compare patterns

> I am going down to the <u>shops</u>.
>
> 我要上街去。

> I need to go to the <u>store</u> for some milk.
>
> 我需要去商店買些牛奶。

Try the test

☐   1.   He does not like going to department shops.

☐   2.   I am just going down to the shops.

1. ✗   2. ✓

28　比較 since、on

收到一家公司的來信，説將於七月一日搬遷，*We will move since 1 July.，這是常犯的錯誤。move 是 "公司搬遷、人搬家" 的意思。例如：

The company is moving to the New Territories.

公司準備遷往新界。

She moved house last week.

她上星期搬了家。

但若有搬遷日期，我們應説 on。例如：

He will move in on the first of next month.

他將於下個月一號搬進去。

因此，説 "我們將於七月一日搬遷。"，應是 We will move on 1 July.。

> Note：since 常與主句中的 perfect tense 連用。例如：
>
> They have been waiting here since two o'clock.
> 他們從兩點鐘開始就在這裏等候了。
> She has known about it since April.
> 她從四月份起就知道了這事。

Compare patterns

We are moving next week.

我們下星期搬家。

Everything has changed since last June.

自從去年六月以來一切都變了。

Try the test

☐　1. It hasn't rained since July.

☐　2. They will move since December.

1. ✓　2. ✗

29   太多 little mistakes 就不是 small mistakes

small 用於具體事物，表達 "量、大小、尺寸、數量、價值、重要性" 等方面的 "小"。其反義詞是 big, large。a <u>small</u> sum of money 是 "一小筆錢"，而 <u>small</u> mistakes 是 "小錯誤"。

它可以放在名詞前面，或 Be 動詞的後面。例如：

> Portable computers need to be <u>small</u>.
> 手提電腦要小型。

little 是 "小巧、微小" 的意思，指與正常標準相差極遠，可表示說話人是否喜歡，通常只放在名詞前面。例如：

> What is the name of that <u>little</u> red flower?
> 那朵小紅花名字叫甚麼？

> Look at that poor <u>little</u> boy.
> 你看那可憐的男孩。

> Why do you come up to me with every <u>little</u> difficulty?
> 你為何一點小困難就來找我？

因此，small girl 是 "個子小的女孩"，而 little girl 是 "年紀小的女孩"。

> Note：little 用作形容詞時，前面不用 very 或 too。例如：我們不說 *I have a very little car. 或 *Our house is very little.。而 little 前面可用其他形容詞如 a nice little man。

Compare patterns

> There are some <u>small</u> mistakes in your letters.
> 你信裏有些小錯誤。

> Your letter is full of <u>little</u> mistakes.
> 你信裏充滿各種小錯誤。

Try the test

☐   1. Look at that poor little girl.

☐   2. I have a little sum of money.

1. ✓   2. ✗

30　spend 搭配名詞，不後接 to

首先，spend 是 "用、花（錢）" 的意思。例如：

She <u>has spent</u> all her money already.

她已花光自己全部的錢。

I <u>spent</u> $1,000 on a new dress.

我花一千元買了一條新連衣裙。

The company <u>has spent</u> a lot of money updating their computer systems.

公司花了很多錢更新電腦系統。

其次，spend 是 "花時間、度過" 的意思。例如：

They <u>spent</u> the weekend in Japan.

他們在日本度過了週末。

How long did he <u>spend</u> on his homework?

他用了多長時間做功課？

She <u>spends</u> too much time watching television.

她花太多時間看電視。

> Note：*He spent the evening <u>to write</u> a letter. 是錯的，應說 He spent the evening <u>writing</u> a letter.。

Compare patterns

He <u>spends</u> too much effort on things that don't matter.

他在一些無關緊要的事上花太多精力。

My daughter <u>is spending</u> the night with a friend.

我女兒要在一個朋友那裏過夜。

Try the test

☐　1.　They spend a lot of money on advertising.

☐　2.　He spent three years on prison.

1. ✓　2. ✗

31   似同非同：start 和 begin

start 和 begin 都是 "開始發生或存在" 的意思。例如：

> When does the class <u>start</u>?
>
> 甚麼時候上課？
>
> When does the concert <u>begin</u>?
>
> 音樂會甚麼時候開始？

其實，start 和 begin 差別不大。start 較常用於英語口語和商業語境，begin 較常用於英語書面語，描述一系列事情。例如：

> The story <u>begins</u> on an island of Cook.
>
> 故事以科克島開始。

start 指 "開動機器、開車"。例如：

> The car won't <u>start</u>.
>
> 這輛車發動不起來。

> Note：start 有些特別用法。例如：get started 是 "使開始、着手、動手" 的意思。例如：
>
> It's nine o'clock. Let's <u>get started</u>.
>
> 快九點了，我們開始吧。

Compare patterns

> <u>Has</u> the meeting <u>started</u> yet?
>
> 會議開始了嗎？
>
> I will <u>begin</u> whenever you are ready.
>
> 你何時準備好我就開始。

Try the test

- ☐   1. The lorry did not begin.
- ☐   2. We will begin by dancing.

1. ✗   2. ✓

32 "送人回家"別說錯"帶人回家"

在節日派對或聚會結束時，開車的朋友常客氣地問其他賓客，要不要坐他們的車回家。記着要説 Can I take you home? 而不是 *Can I bring you home?，因為 bring you home 是帶人回自己的家。請看其他例子：

A waiter <u>took</u> us to our room.

服務員帶我們到房間。

I <u>am taking</u> the kids swimming later.

我遲些帶孩子們去游泳。

總之，take 是"送 / 帶 / 拿走到一個遠離説話人的地方"，而 bring 是"送 / 帶 / 拿到説話人的地方"。請看其他例子：

Don't forget to <u>take</u> your bag when you go.

走的時候別忘了拿你的袋。

Please <u>bring</u> your calculator every lesson.

請你每次上課帶你的計算機。

I often forget to <u>take</u> my umbrella.

我常忘了帶雨傘。

Compare patterns

Can I <u>take</u> you home?

我可以送你回家嗎？

Can I <u>bring</u> you home?

我可以帶你回家嗎？

Try the test

☐　1.　I am bringing the kids swimming.

☐　2.　A waiter took us to the room.

1. ✗　2. ✓

33   表達感謝有多種方式

學好英語方法多於困難。

很多人對學英語已採取放棄態度，只因為不知道學英語的方法，其實英語不難學，只要方法正確，多多練習，注意不要犯錯，就會越來越好。

說"謝謝"時，thanks 比 thank you 更隨便，像 <u>Thanks</u> for the lift. 和 <u>Thanks</u> for helping out.。

"感謝你"是 Thank you.，不是 Thanks you.。例如：<u>Thank you</u> for a delicious dinner. 和 <u>Thank you</u> for the ring, Peter.。

"非常感謝"是 Thank you very much.；"太感謝你"是 Thanks very much. 或 Thanks a lot.，不是 *Thank you a lot. 或 *Thanks lots.。

說"感謝上帝，到星期六了。"，是 <u>Thank goodness</u> it is Saturday.，不是 *Thanks goodness it is Saturday.。

說"真是太感謝你了"是 <u>Thank you very much</u> indeed.，不是 *Thank you indeed.。

> Note：Thank you for... / Thanks for... 可後跟 -ing 形式。例如"謝謝你光臨。" 是 <u>Thank you for</u> coming.，不是 *Thank you for your coming.。

Try to remember

More Informal　較非正式	More Formal　較正式
Thanks.	Thank you.
Thanks a lot.	Thank you very much.
Thanks a lot indeed.	Thank you very much indeed.
Thanks for coming.	Thank you for coming.

Try the test

☐　1. Thank you very much indeed.

☐　2. Thank you for your coming.

☐　3. Thanks goodness.

☐　4. Thank you a lot.

1. ✓　2. ✗　3. ✗　4. ✗

34 似同非同：trouble 和 problem

有 trouble 是有問題、麻煩、憂慮。

problem 表示 "引起困難需要處理的情況"。它是可數名詞。例如：

Tell me what the problem is.

告訴我問題是甚麼。

There is a problem with the engine.

發動機出了問題。

She is having a few problems at work.

她工作出了些問題。

口語的 No problem 是 "沒問題"。

trouble 表示 "問題、困難、憂慮"，泛指 "問題難以解決"，幾乎始終用作不可數名詞。例如：

We had some trouble while we were on holiday.

度假時我們遇到了一些麻煩。

She helped me when I was in trouble.

我遇到困難時她幫過我。

He had trouble with the car last night.

昨晚他的車出了問題。

Compare patterns

She is having a few problems at work.

她工作出了些問題。

He had trouble with the car last night.

昨晚他的車出了問題。

Try the test

☐   1. There is a problem with the engine.

☐   2. She helped me when I was in problem.

1. ✓   2. ✗

35   unlike 與 "喜歡" 無關

社交網站常出現 like，解作 "喜歡"。但注意反義詞是 dislike，不是 unlike。

dislike 是 "不喜歡、不喜愛、討厭" 的意思，它是動詞，也是名詞。例如：

> Why do you dislike him so much?
> 你為何那麼討厭他呢？

> He dislikes having to get up so early.
> 他討厭很早就要起牀。

> She has a dislike of / for cats.
> 她不喜歡貓。

unlike 是 "不像"、"和……不同" 的意思。例如：

> She is very unlike her mother.
> 她很不像她母親。

> Unlike most systems, this one is easy to install.
> 本系統與大多數系統不同，它極容易安裝。

Compare patterns

> Why do you dislike him so much?
> 你為何那麼討厭他？

> She is very unlike her mother.
> 她很不像她母親。

Try the test

☐   1. He unlikes having to get up so early.

☐   2. Unlike most systems, this one is easy to install.

☐   3. Why do you unlike him so much?

1. ✗   2. ✓   3. ✗

II

Common sentence patterns
常用句式

36   all of a sudden 突然

我們寫記敘文時，特別是描述故事人物的動作或事情的發生，常説 "突然、突然之間、突如其來、出乎意料、一下子"，除了 suddenly 之外，還可説 all of a sudden。它也是 "猛然、猛地、猛不防" 的意思。例如：

All of a sudden someone grabbed me around the neck.

冷不防有人抓住了我的脖子。

It seemed to happen all of a sudden —I felt dizzy and I just collapsed.

一切似乎都發生得很突然 —— 我覺得頭暈後就暈倒了。

All of a sudden the lights went out.

突然，所有燈都熄滅了。

All of a sudden he didn't look sleepy any more.

突然，他看上去不再憊憊欲睡了。

Try to remember

All of a sudden, the bedroom window flew open.

突然，睡房窗戶被風吹開。

All of a sudden, there was a knock on the door.

突然，有人敲門。

Similar patterns

I suddenly realized what I had to do.

我突然明白我該怎麼做。

It all happened so suddenly.

一切都發生得那麼突然。

Try the test

☐　1. All of sudden, there came a knock to the door.

☐　2. It all happened so suddenly.

1. ×　2. ✓

37　as a matter of fact 事實上

在議論文裏，我們常説 in fact, as a matter of fact，來強調意見或提到的相反意見，即 "事實上、實際上、其實" 的意思。例如：

I thought the work would be difficult. <u>In fact</u>, it's very easy.

我原以為這工作很難。事實上它很容易。

It's a nice place. We have stayed there ourselves, <u>as a matter of fact</u>.

那地方不錯。其實，我們自己在那裏逗留過。

<u>As a matter of fact</u>, I have the telephone number written down somewhere.

實際上，我把那電話號碼寫在某地方。

> Note：The fact is 是 "實際情況是" 的意思。例如：
>
> A new car would be wonderful but <u>the fact is</u> we can't afford one.
> 有新車好是好，不過實際的情況是，我們買不起。

Try to remember

I haven't been here long. <u>As a matter of fact</u>, I just got off the plane last night.

我到這裏沒多久。實際上，我昨天晚上剛下飛機。

I guess you haven't eaten yet. <u>As a matter of fact</u>, I have.

我猜你還沒吃飯。其實，我已吃過了。

Similar patterns

I don't like him; <u>in fact</u>, I hate him.

我不喜歡他，事實上，我憎厭他。

I don't have a car. <u>In fact</u>, I can't drive.

我沒有車，事實上，我也不會開車。

Try the test

☐   1. As a matter of fact, I was the one who did it.

☐   2. As a fact, Peter was right.

1. ✓   2. ✗

38   as a result 因此

我們用英文作文時，常引用因果關係説明某行動導致某結果。為增加文章説服力，也會説明某事或某情況由某原因引起。其中一個常用語是 as a result，同義詞是 because of，是"由於、因為、因此"的意思。例如：

Profits have declined <u>as a result</u> of the recent drop in sales.
由於近來銷量下跌，利潤下降了。

He died <u>as a result</u> of his injuries.
他因傷而死。

She made a big mistake, and <u>as a result</u>, lost her job.
她犯了個大錯，結果丟了工作。

The failure of the company was <u>a</u> direct <u>result</u> of bad management.
公司失敗的直接原因是管理不善。

Try to remember

King's Road will be closed and delays are likely <u>as a result</u>.
英皇道快將封閉，很可能會造成延誤。

He was late as <u>a result of</u> the snow.
他因下雪來遲了。

Similar patterns

She walked slowly <u>because of</u> her bad leg.
她因腿不方便走路緩慢。

I stayed at home <u>because of</u> the heavy rain.
我因下大雨留在家裏。

Try the test

☐   1. She is unable to go to work as result of the fall from her horse.

☐   2. The fire was the result of carelessness.

1. ✗   2. ✓

39   as far as...is concerned 就⋯⋯而言

如果要發表對某事的意見，可以説 As far as I am concerned。例如：

As far as I am concerned, you can do what you like.

就我而言，你想做甚麼就可以做甚麼。

As far as I am concerned, the whole idea is crazy.

依我之見，整個想法真是荒誕之極。

除了自己，我們還可以談論事物。例如：

As far as stability is concerned, a change of government would be a good idea.

就穩定而言，更換政府會是個好主意。

> Note：too far 是 "過份" 的意思。例如：
> The police went too far when they arrested the protesters.
> 警察把抗議人士拘捕的做法太過份了。

Try to remember

As far as we are concerned, you can go whenever you want.

就我們而言，你們隨時想走都可以。

As far as I'm concerned, the officials incited the fight.

在我看來，是這些官員煽動起這場爭鬥。

Similar patterns

In my opinion, the whole idea is not bad.

我認為整個想法不差。

In my opinion, he is wrong.

依我看，他錯了。

Try the test

☐   1. As far as he was concerned, things were going well.

☐   2. As far as your family's concern, you won't have to worry about them any longer.

1. ✓   2. ✗

40   as long as 只要

怎樣可提高英語水平呢？其中一個方法是在日常生活裏多練習常用的英語。哪些是常用英語呢？as long as 是一個好例子，是"只要"的意思，同義詞是 so long as。例如：

You can go as long as you are home for dinner.
只要你回家吃飯，你就可以去。

Bring your friends by all means—just as long as I know how many are coming.
一定要把你的朋友帶來 —— 只要讓我知道有多少人來就行。

I can come as long as I can leave by 5:00.
只要我能在 5 點鐘之前離開，我就能來。

Try to remember

You can borrow the book as long as you return it to me next week.
你可以借這本書，只要你下星期還給我就行。

You can go out, as long as you promised to be back before 10 o'clock.
你可以出去，只要你答應十時前回來。

Similar patterns

We will go so long as the weather is good.
只要天氣好，我們就去。

So long as there is a demand, supply will be there.
只要有需求，供應也就存在。

Try the test

☐   1. I don't care, so as long as I can stay.

☐   2. As long as you are happy, it doesn't matter what you do.

1. ✗   2. ✓

41   ...as soon as... 一……就……

學英語時應多用在中文也同樣常用的簡單用語，如中文常説 " 一 ……
就…… "，英文是 as soon as，同義詞是 once。例如：

She got married <u>as soon as</u> she left school.

她中學一畢業就結婚了。

<u>As soon as</u> I saw him, I knew there was something wrong.

我一看到他就知道出事了。

We need the repairs done <u>as soon as</u> possible.

我們需要盡快修理好。

'When would you like to meet?' '<u>The sooner the better.</u>'

"你想甚麼時候見面？" "越快越好。"

If you cheat, you will be found out <u>sooner or later</u>.

如果你作弊，遲早被人發現。

Try to remember

He got married <u>as soon as</u> he found a job.

他一找到工作就結婚了。

You will never guess what happened <u>as soon as</u> I left the office.

你怎麼也想不到，我一離開辦公室就發生了甚麼事。

Similar patterns

<u>Once</u> he arrives, we can start.

他一來，我們就可以開始。

<u>Once</u> in bed, the children usually fall asleep easily.

小孩一旦上了牀，通常很快睡着。

Try the test

☐ 1. You may go as soon as she gets home.

☐ 2. As soon I got home, my sister went out.

1. ✔   2. ✗

42   for example 例如

用 for example 或 for instance 舉例說明論點時，常會犯錯，首先，必須注意無論有多少個例子，它們只有單數，沒有複數。例如：

> Many countries, <u>for example</u> Japan, Taiwan and China, often have earthquakes.
> 許多國家，例如日本、台灣和中國經常發生地震。

其次，在一個句子後面可以用大寫 for example，加上逗號，再在後面寫一個完整句子。例如：

> Cars price can vary a lot. <u>For example</u>, in Britain the VW Golf costs $1,000 more than in Belgium.
> 汽車價錢差距可以很大，例如在英國，VW Golf 的價錢較在比利時高 $1,000 美元。

Try to remember

> A lot of us want to leave now, <u>for example</u>, Peter.
> 我們當中有許多人想現在就走，例如彼得。

> It is extremely expensive to live in Hong Kong. <u>For example</u>, I pay $10,000 for a two-room flat.
> 在香港居住真是太貴了。比如說，租一個兩房單位我要支付一萬元。

Similar patterns

> You can't rely on him; <u>for instance</u>, he was absent yesterday.
> 他這個人靠不住。舉例說吧，他昨天就缺席了。

> What would you do, <u>for instance</u>, if you find a student stealing?
> 比如說，如果你發現有學生偷東西，你會怎樣處理？

Try the test

☐   1. A lot of people here, for examples, Peter and Susan, would rather like coffee.

☐   2. China, Japan and Canada, for example, all have oil reserves.

1. ✗   2. ✓

43   for the time being 暫時

time 有很多短語，例如 for the time being ，是 "暫時、目前" 的意思，同義詞是 for the moment。例如：

She can stay with us for the time being until she finds a place of her own.
在她找到住處之前，可以暫住我們這裏。

Now, for the time being, he is living with his father in Japan.
他暫時和父親住在日本。

You can leave your luggage here for the time being.
你可以暫時把行李留在這裏。

It is not perfect but it is good enough for the time being.
雖然說不上十全十美，但目前看來已夠好了。

I am happy here for the moment, but I might want to move soon.
目前，我在這裏過得不錯，但我可能不久就想去別的地方。

Try to remember

Can you share a room for the time being?
你可以暫時跟人合住一個房間嗎？

Leave the cleaning for the time being — please do it later.
暫且放下清潔工作 —— 請你遲些做。

Similar patterns

For the moment, we are willing to watch and wait.
目前我們願意在一旁觀察和等待。

Let's carry on with what we agreed for the moment.
目前我們繼續做雙方同意的部分。

Try the test

☐   1. That's enough for the time being.

☐   2. For the being time, you have to share this room with your brother.

1. ✓   2. ✗

44   generally speaking 總的來說

我從事英語教學多年，一向認為不懂英語語法規則就不能準確表達意思。不過，很多人現在已習慣中英夾雜或中式英語，對英語語法得過且過，例如，有人會混淆：

	錯誤搭配		正確搭配	
坦白	Frank		Frankly	
大體上	Broad		Broadly	
從歷史的角度看	Historical		Historically	
嚴格地	Strict	speaking	Strictly	speaking
粗略	Rough		Roughly	
相對	Relative		Relatively	
個人	Personal		Personally	
一般來説	General		Generally	

原因很簡單：因為 speaking 是動詞，我們要用副詞修飾動詞。

Try to remember

Generally speaking, it is quite a good school.

總的來説，這是一所不錯的學校。

Strictly speaking, I should report to the general manager.

嚴格來説，我應該向總經理報告這件事。

Similar patterns

Broadly speaking, I agree with you.

我大體上認同你。

Relatively speaking, men make better drivers than women.

相對來説，男性開車比女性開得好。

Try the test

☐   1. General speaking, the performance is good.

☐   2. Strictly speaking, that school is not very old.

1. ✗   2. ✓

45　from time to time 不時

time 有很多實用的慣用語和短語。for the time being 是 "暫時" 的意思。
例如：

> You can leave your coat here <u>for the time being</u>.
>
> 你可以暫時把大衣放這裏。

from time to time 是 "不時" 的意思，同義詞是 sometimes。例如：

> She has to work on / at weekends <u>from time to time</u>.
>
> 她不時需要週末工作。

take your time 是 "從容不迫、慢慢來" 的意思。例如：

> There is no rush — <u>take your time</u>.
>
> 不急的，慢慢來。

time off 是 "休息"。例如：

> She never takes any <u>time off</u>.
>
> 她從不休息。

Time is up. 是 "時間到了。"。例如：

> <u>Time is up</u> — pens down.
>
> 時間到了，請停筆。

以下是含 time 的慣用語：

be living on borrowed time	苟且存活
call time on something	結束某事
have time on your hands	不知如何打發過多的空閒時間
hit the big time	飛黃騰達
in no time	馬上
mark time	按兵不動，靜觀其變
play for time	以行動或言語拖延，以爭取時間做最佳打算

Try to remember

They come to see us <u>from time to time</u>.

他們有時過來看我們。

<u>From time to time</u>, I still think of him.

我有時還會想起他。

Similar patterns

<u>Sometimes</u> I come by train, <u>but usually</u> I come by car.

有時我乘火車來，但通常我乘汽車。

<u>Sometimes</u> it is best not to say anything.

有時最好是甚麼都不說。

Try the test

☐   1. I'll see you time to time.

☐   2. She sent money to him from time to time for a year.

1. ✗   2. ✓

46 in case of 假使

在正式通告表達"如果、假使"，可以用 in case of。常見例子是：

> In case of fire, ring the alarm bell.
>
> 如發生火災，即按響警鐘。

> In case of bad weather, the reception will be held indoors.
>
> 萬一下雨，招待會將在室內舉行。

在美國，in case 也是"如果、假使"的意思。例如：

> In case they are late, we can always sit in the bar.
>
> 如果他們遲到，我們總可以在酒吧裏坐一坐。

Note：just in case 是"以防、以防萬一"的意思。例如：
> Take the umbrella in case it rains / (just) in case it should rain.
> 帶着雨傘吧，以防（萬一）下雨。

Try to remember

> In case you can't come, give me a call before I leave for work.
>
> 如果你來不了，在我上班前給我打個電話。

> I don't think I'll need any money but I'll bring some just in case.
>
> 我想我不會用到錢的，不過我還是要帶一些以防萬一。

Similar patterns

> In case of need, I can make a trip to Japan.
>
> 如有需要，我可以去日本一趟。

> Bring a map in case you get lost.
>
> 帶張地圖吧，以防迷路。

Try the test

☐   1. I keep an umbrella here in case of rain.

☐   2. In case of I forget, please remind me about it.

1. ✓   2. ✗

47   in the same way 同樣地

說完一個論點後再說另一個同樣觀點時，可以說 in the same way。例如：

> There is no reason why a gifted aircraft designer should also be a capable pilot. <u>In the same way</u>, a brilliant pilot can be a menace behind the wheel of a car.
> 很有天份的飛機設計師沒理由也會是個好機師。同樣，一名優秀的機師坐在汽車方向盤前可能會構成危險。

Try to remember

> Every baby's face is different from every other's. <u>In the same way</u>, every baby's pattern of development is different from every other's.
> 嬰孩每張臉都不同。同樣，嬰孩的發育模式也因人而異。

Similar patterns

> Men must wear a suit, <u>similarly</u>, women must wear a skirt.
> 男士必須穿西裝。同樣，女士必須穿裙子。

> Chinese won most of the track and field events. <u>Similarly</u>, in swimming, the top three places went to Chinese.
> 中國隊在田徑賽大多項目裏大獲全勝。同樣，在游泳方面中國也囊括了前三名。

Try the test

☐   1. Boys wear fashionable clothes. Similarly, some birds have bright feathers.

☐   2. The girls are similar dressed.

1. ✓   2. ✗

48 instead 反而

多用轉折詞有助作文流暢。以下是時間轉折詞：

when	until
before	the moment
after	five minutes later
shortly afterwards	

至於補充、讓步、原因、後果等詞組也很有用。例如，instead 是 "反而、代替、卻" 的意思，它的同義詞是 rather than。例如：

Peter was ill so I went instead.

彼得病了，所以我（代他）去了。

She didn't reply. Instead, she turned on her heel and left the room.

她沒回答，反而轉身離開了房間。

If you don't want to go, I'll go instead.

你要是不打算去，我就替你去好了。

> Note：instead 加上 of 是 "代替" 的意思。例如：
>
> Now I can walk to school instead of going by bus.
> 現在我可以步行上學，不必坐公車了。

Try to remember

There is no coffee — would you like a cup of tea instead?

沒有咖啡，可否來杯茶？

Instead of throwing away your household rubbish, why not recycle it?

與其扔掉家裏的垃圾，何不循環再用呢？

Similar patterns

I think I'd like to stay at home this evening <u>rather than</u> going out.

我想今晚我情願留在家裏也不想外出。

He likes starting early <u>rather than</u> staying late.

他喜歡早動身而不是留到很晚。

Try the test

☐   1. Last summer, I went to Italy. This year, I'm going to France instead.

☐   2. I will go instead you.

1. ✓   2. ✗

49   ...more and more... ······越來越······

形容某情況發生變化，程度加劇或數量增加，可以說 ...more and more... ，即 "······越來越······" 同義詞是 the more...the more...。例如：

The questions get <u>more and more</u> difficult.

問題越來越難。

We seem to spend <u>more and more</u> on food every month!

我們每月花在食物上的錢似乎越來越多了！

I find myself thinking about it <u>more and more</u>.

我發覺自己越來越多考慮那件事。

Peter became <u>more and more</u> furious.

彼得變得越來越憤怒了。

Try to remember

<u>More and more</u> people grew ill.

越來越多人生了病。

We became <u>more and more</u> friendly to Susan.

我們對蘇珊越來越友好了。

Similar patterns

<u>The more</u> he drank, <u>the more</u> violent he became.

他喝得越醉，越變得狂暴。

It always seems like <u>the more</u> I earn, <u>the more</u> I spend.

我好像錢賺得越多，花得越多。

Try the test

☐   1. The story gets more more exciting.

☐   2. Indeed, she liked him more and more.

1. ✗   2. ✓

50　no matter 無論

"無論、不管" 英文是 no matter，必須與 what, which, where, who, whose, when, whether 及 how 連用 no matter 的同義詞是 regardless。例如：

I'll love you no matter what you do.
無論你做甚麼，我都會一樣愛你。

No matter where you go, you'll find Coca Cola.
不管你走到哪裏，都會看到可口可樂。

You'll be welcome no matter when you come.
隨時歡迎你來。

The law requires equal treatment for all, regardless of race, religion, or sex.
法律規定人人平等，不分種族、宗教或性別。

> Note：no matter who / what 的用法和 whoever, whatever 很相像。例如：
> Whatever / No matter what you say, I won't believe you.
> 不管你說甚麼，我決不信你。

no matter what 放在句尾時 = no matter what happens。例如：

I'll never give up, no matter what.
我不會放棄，不管發生甚麼事。

Try to remember

We have to get the car fixed, no matter how much it costs.
無論花多少錢，我們也要把車修理好。

Feeding a baby is a messy job no matter how careful you are.
餵嬰孩吃東西，無論怎樣小心都很麻煩。

Similar patterns

The plan for a new office tower went ahead <u>regardless of</u> local opposition.

儘管受到當地人反對，新辦公大樓的興建計劃仍如期進行。

Try the test

☐   1. No matter happened, he would not say a word.

☐   2. You can't go in no matter who you are.

1. ✗   2. ✓

51   no sooner...than...   一……就……

我們敍述故事時，常把兩個已完成的行動作出比較，以便別人看到動作的緊湊，留下深刻印象。當然，我們完成一個行動後，可以用 then 或 afterwards 説出另一行動，例如 She had said it. Then she burst into tears. ，但這可能有點平鋪直敍。但如果改説 No sooner had she said it than she burst into tears. 即 "她一説完淚水就奪眶而出。" ，動作和形象就會生動突出。其他例子還有：

No sooner had we sat down at the table than the phone rang.
我們剛在桌子旁坐下，電話就響了起來。

> Note：全句應該用過去式，並必須使用過去完成式 (past perfect tense)，描述較早完成的事。

Try to remember

No sooner had I started mowing the lawn than it started raining.
我剛開始剪草就下起雨。

No sooner had we sat down than we found it was time to go.
我們剛坐下就發現是時候要走。

no sooner...than... 的同義詞是 scarcely...when...。

Similar patterns

Scarcely had we arrived when we had to leave again.
我們剛到就要離開。

I had scarcely sat down to eat when the phone rang.
我剛坐下吃飯，電話就響了起來。

Try the test

☐   1. No sooner had he gone to sleep than the telephone rang once more.

☐   2. He no soon reached the door than he came back.

1. ✓   2. ✗

52   not only...(but) also... 不但……而且……

要英文寫得好，除了注意語法和詞彙外，還要懂得基本句型。若要寫 300 字，除了引言和總結，寫四段就可以，即一段大約 60 字，not only...(but) also... 就屬於基本句型，同義詞是 too。例如：

We go there <u>not only</u> in summer, <u>but also</u> in winter.
我們不但夏天去那裏，冬天也去。

<u>Not only</u> the toilet was flooded, <u>but also</u> the sitting room.
不但洗手間裏滿是水，客廳也全是。

The place was <u>not only</u> cold, <u>but also</u> damp.
那地方冰冷潮濕。

She <u>not only</u> plays the piano, <u>but also</u> the violin.
她不但彈鋼琴，還拉小提琴。

Try to remember

<u>Not only</u> did she turned up late, <u>but</u> she <u>also</u> forgot her books.
她不但遲到，還忘了帶書。

If our application is not successful, it will affect <u>not only</u> our department, <u>but also</u> the whole company.
如果申請不成功，不僅影響到我們部門，還影響到全公司。

Similar patterns

I can dance. I can sing too.
我會跳舞，也會唱歌。

Susan has got a lovely voice — she is a pretty good dancer too.
蘇珊聲音很甜美，舞跳得也不錯。

Try the test

☐   1. Not only my mother was unhappy, but Mary.

☐   2. Not only did he speak more correctly, but he spoke more easily.

1. ✗   2. ✓

53   of your own accord 自願地

表達自願或主動做一件事或採取行動，英語是 of your own accord。例如：

> He left the meeting of his own accord.
> 他主動離開會場。

> I didn't need to tell him to apologise; he did it of his own accord.
> 不需要我告訴他，他主動道了歉。

> The door seemed to move of its own accord.
> 那扇門似乎自己在動。

> The symptoms will clear up of their own accord.
> 病徵將自行消失。

> In many cases the disease will clear up of its own accord.
> 這種病在許多情況下會自動痊癒。

Try to remember

> She decided to let him alone until he stopped of his own accord.
> 她決定不去管他，等他自動停止。

> In the end, they knew he would leave of his own accord.
> 他們知道最後他會自願離開。

Similar patterns

> I would willingly help you if I weren't going away tomorrow.
> 如果我明天不走的話，我會很樂意幫助你的。

> People would willingly pay more for better services.
> 人願意多花些錢去享受較好的服務。

Try the test

☐   1. Susan came of her own accord.

☐   2. He did it of own accord.

1. ✓   2. ✗

54   On the one hand 一方面

我們討論、交換意見、提出不同甚至於對立的觀點，會說 On the one hand...on the other (hand)...，即 "一方面……，另一方面……"。例如：

> On the one hand, he'd love to have more income, but on the other hand, he doesn't want to give up his freedom.
>
> 一方面他想要多些收入，另一方面他又不想放棄自由自在的生活。
>
> On the one hand, I'd like a job which pays more, but on the other hand, I enjoy the work I'm doing at the moment.
>
> 一方面我想要更高薪的工作，另一方面我又喜歡現在的工作。

Try to remember

> He has caught in a dispute between the city council on the one hand and the Education Bureau on the other.
>
> 他捲入了一場市議會和教育局之間的爭議。
>
> On the one hand, they'd love to have kids, but on the other, they don't want to give up their freedom.
>
> 一方面他們想要孩子，另一方面他們又不想放棄自由。

Similar patterns

> While I accept that he is not perfect in many respects, I do actually quite like the man.
>
> 雖然我承認他不是十全十美，但我真的非常喜歡這個人。
>
> While I fully understand your point of view, I do also have some sympathy with Peter's.
>
> 儘管我完全理解你的觀點，但我有點認同彼得。

Try the test

☐   1. On one hand, I admire his courage, but on the other I distrust his judgment.

☐   2. On the one hand you accept her presents; on the other, you are rude to the whole family. What really is your attitude to them?

1. ✗   2. ✓

55   sooner or later 遲早

説未確定但將會發生的事，英語是 sooner or later。同義詞是 some / one day，例如：

His wife is bound to find out <u>sooner or later</u>.
他太太遲早會發現的。

<u>Sooner or later</u> you have to make a decision.
你早晚得拿個主意。

Don't worry, <u>sooner or later</u> she will come home.
別着急，她遲早會回家的。

> Note：sooner rather than later 是 "及早、趕早不趕晚" 的意思。例如：
> We urged her to sort out the problem <u>sooner rather than later</u>.
> 我們敦促她及早解決那個問題。

Try to remember

<u>Sooner or later</u> he is going to realize what a mistake he has made.
他遲早意識到自己犯了一個多嚴重的錯誤。

If you cheat, you'll be found out <u>sooner or later</u>.
你如果作弊，遲早總會被發現。

Similar patterns

We'll take a trip to Japan <u>some / one day</u>.
總有一天，我們會到日本旅行。

<u>Some / one day</u> I'll be famous.
總有一天，我會成名的。

Try the test

☐   1. Soon or late, she will know the truth.

☐   2. They will create trouble sooner or later.

1. ✗   2. ✓

56　To my surprise 使我驚訝

對突如其來或有特別感覺的事物，可在句子開頭説 To my / her / his (great) surprise / astonishment... 。例如：

To my great surprise, I passed.
使我大為驚訝的是，我及格了。

Much to his surprise, they offered him the job.
使他甚為驚奇的是，他們聘請了他。

To everyone's surprise, the plan succeeded.
出乎每個人意料之外，那個計劃成功了。

To her astonishment, he remembered her name.
使她大為吃驚，他記得她的名字。

To my / her / his / our disappointment... 解作 "大失所望"。

To our great disappointment, it rained every day of the trip.
這次旅行天天下雨，令我們大失所望。

Try to remember

To my great surprise, he agreed to all our demands.
使我非常驚訝的是他答應了我們所有要求。

To my surprise, I found I liked it.
我吃驚地發現自己很喜歡它。

Similar patterns

To the astonishment of her colleagues, she resigned.
她竟然辭職了，這令她同事大吃一驚。

To our astonishment, she actually arrived on time.
使我們大為驚訝的是她竟然準時到。

Try the test

☐　1. To our surprises, he succeeded.

☐　2. To my great surprise, the door was unlocked.

1. ✗　2. ✓

57   ...until...   ……直到……為止

我們常説"等到、直到……為止、直到……才",英文是 until,非正式説
法是 till。例如:

Let's wait <u>until</u> 10 o'clock, but he didn't come.
她一直等到十點鐘,但他仍沒來。

Let's wait <u>until</u> the rain stops.
讓我們等到雨停下來再作打算。

<u>Until</u> he spoke I hadn't realized he wasn't Japanese.
直到他開口説話,我才知道他不是日本人。

You are not going out <u>until</u> you have finished your homework.
你沒做完功課就不准出去 / 你做完功課才准出去。

<u>Until now</u> I have always lived alone.
直到現在,我一直獨自生活。

She continued working up <u>until</u> her death.
她一直工作到去世。

The street is full of traffic from morning <u>till</u> night.
街上從早到晚車水馬龍。

Try to remember

Hadn't we better wait <u>until</u> Peter is here?
我們是不是最好等到彼得來?

You should stay on the train <u>until</u> Admiralty and then change.
你該坐車到金鐘再換車。

until 的同義詞是 up to。

Similar patterns

<u>Up to</u> yesterday, we had no idea where the girl was.
直到昨天,我們還不知道那女孩的下落。

She was here <u>up to</u> a minute ago.
她剛才還一直在這裏。

Try the test

☐   1. They worked until 10 p.m., and then quit.

☐   2. I did not begin work until he has gone.

1. ✓   2. ✗

58   ...what is more...   ……更重要的是……

作文時要加強一個論點或增加更重要的資料，可以用 What is more，即
"更甚、更重要的是、另外、此外、而且"的意思。例如：

I don't like pubs. They are noisy, smelly, and <u>what is more</u>,
expensive.

我不喜歡酒吧。那裏嘈吵，氣味難聞，更重要的是，花費太多。

He admitted he'd spoken to them, and <u>what's more</u> had told them
about our secret discussions.

他承認他和他們講過話，更糟的是把我們秘密討論的內容都告訴
了他們。

These soaps are environmentally friendly; <u>what is more</u>, they are
relatively cheap.

這些肥皂環保，最重要的是價錢較便宜。

You should remember it, and <u>what is more</u>, you should get it right.

你該記住它，此外，更應該把它做好。

Try to remember

The decorations were absolutely beautiful and <u>what is more</u>, the
girls had made them themselves.

那些裝飾絕對很美，更重要的是，它們由那些女孩親手做的。

The new system is cheaper, and <u>what is more</u>, it is better.

這個新系統價錢比較低，更重要的是質量較佳。

what is more 的同義詞是 moreover。

Similar patterns

The whole report is well written. <u>Moreover</u>, it is accurate.

整個報告寫得很好，而且描寫準確。

The rent is reasonable, and <u>moreover</u>, the location is perfect.

這裏房租合理，而且地點非常優越。

Try the test

☐ 1. He came after midnight, and what more, he was drunk.

☐ 2. He was late for class, and what is more, he lost his wallet.

1. ✗   2. ✓

III

Idioms commonly used
常見慣用語

59　a piece of cake 易如反掌

用英語表達"很容易"是 easy，如 an easy job / exam 是"容易的工作 / 考試"，例如：

> It is <u>easy</u> for me to get there.
> 我很容易到那裏。

> Note：a piece of cake 不是"一件西餅"，是強調做事"易如反掌、不費吹灰之力"。

> I need not have worried about my Japanese examination — it was <u>a piece of cake</u>.
> 我本不必擔心我的日語考試 —— 它是不費吹灰之力的事。

> After climbing mountains in the Swiss Alps, going up English hills is <u>a piece of cake</u>.
> 爬過了瑞士的阿爾卑斯山後，爬英國的小山簡直易如反掌。

> Taking the photo should be <u>a piece of cake</u> with the new lens I've got.
> 有了新鏡頭，拍起照來就不費吹灰之力。

與 a piece of cake 意義相同的是 as easy as pie。

Try to remember

> The exam was <u>a piece of cake</u>.
> 考試很簡單。

> Firing him will be <u>a piece of cake</u>.
> 開除他是輕而易舉的事。

Similar idioms

Getting rid of her is <u>as easy as pie</u>.
要擺脫她是輕而易舉的事。

Cooking rice is <u>as easy as pie</u>.
煮飯很簡單。

Try the test

☐   1. Let me do this. It is a piece of cake.

☐   2. It is really a cake. I can fix it in five minutes.

1. ✓   2. ✗

60   add fuel to the fire 火上加油

想說一個人的某行動將激怒其他人，並把事情弄得更惡化，中文成語是
"火上加油"，英文也有類似慣用語，那是 add fuel to the flames / fire。
例子：

Threats will only <u>add fuel to the fire</u>.
威脅將只能把事情惡化。

Nothing could help her when she became worried: words of
encouragement just <u>added fuel to the flames</u>.
當她變得煩惱時，再幫她也無補於事。講鼓勵她的話只會火上加
油。

The workers weren't satisfied with their wages, and when they
were asked to work longer hours, it <u>added fuel to the fire</u>.
工人已不滿意他們的工資，要他們延長工時會令他們更不滿。

Try to remember

Her tactless remarks just <u>added fuel to the fire</u>.

她那些沒有技巧的話簡直是火上加油。

The discovery that he was aware of the cover-up has really <u>added fuel to the fire</u>.

人們發現他對隱瞞事件早已知情，這真是火上加油。

Similar idioms

His remarks simply <u>added fuel to the flames</u> of her rage.

他的話只是給她的憤怒火上澆油。

His refusal to apologize just <u>added fuel to the flames</u>.

他不肯道歉只是火上澆油。

Try the test

□　1. Peter was angry with Susan and Susan added flames to the fuel by laughing at him.

□　2. By criticising his son's girl, the father added fuel to the flames of his son's love.

1. ✗　2. ✓

61   as easy as ABC 易如反掌

寫描寫文和記敘文時，對於人或事物，我們常用比喻來達至更生動的效果，英語是 as...as... 。例如：

You're <u>as tall as</u> your father.
你和你父親一樣高。

He doesn't earn <u>as much as</u> me.
他賺的錢比我少。

It's not <u>as hard as</u> I thought.
這沒有我想像的那麼困難。

He was <u>as white as</u> a sheet.
他面無血色。

Peter is <u>as strong as</u> an ox.
彼得強壯得像頭牛。

The woman is <u>as ugly as</u> an owl.
那女人樣子很醜。

我們説做某事易如反掌、輕而易舉或不費吹灰之力，英文是 as easy as ABC / as pie / as anything / as falling off a log。

Try to remember

Her skin is <u>as soft as</u> a baby's.
她的皮膚像嬰兒一樣嬌嫩。

She is <u>as pretty as</u> her sister.
她像她姐姐一樣漂亮。

Similar idioms

I can't run <u>as fast as</u> you.
我沒你跑得快。

It's not <u>as good as</u> it used to be.
這個不如以前好了。

Try the test

☐   1. They say Mary is ugly as an owl.

☐   2. They say Mary is as ugly as an owl.

1. ✗   2. ✓

62   call a spade a spade 有碗話碗

"有碗話碗、有碟話碟"是"直説、實話實説、直言不諱"的意思。英語
是 Call a spade a spade。例如：

> That old man hates long fancy words — he <u>has</u> always <u>called a spade a spade</u>.
>
> 那個長者恨惡長篇漂亮的言辭 —— 他説話一向實話實説。
>
> Let's <u>call a spade a spade</u>. Peter; the man's a thief.
>
> 彼得，我們有話直説吧。這個人是個賊。
>
> She's one politician who tells the truth. In her speeches, she can be depended upon to <u>call a spade a spade</u>.
>
> 她是個講老實話的那種政治家。在她多次演説中，可以信得過她
> 是有碗話碗、有碟話碟的。

Try to remember

> I believe in <u>calling a spade a spade</u>.
>
> 我相信實話實説。
>
> She's not afraid to <u>call a spade a spade</u>.
>
> 她不怕實話實説。

call a spade a spade 的同義詞是 to tell the truth。

Similar idioms

To tell the truth, I was frightened to death.

老實説，我怕得要死。

To tell the truth, I was really very annoyed.

老實説，我真是很惱火。

Try the test

☐   1. A man took some money from Peter's desk and said he borrowed it,
         but I told him he stole it; I believe in calling a spade a spade.

☐   2. A man took some money from Peter's desk and said he borrowed it,
         but I told him he stole it; I believe in calling it a spade.

1. ✓   2. ✗

63　call it a day 到此為止

每天或每次工作時，在停止工作離開工作崗位時可以說 " 今天的工作到此為止。" ，英文是 call it a day ，即 "收工" 。例如：

It's getting pretty late — let's call it a day.

今天已不早，我們就做到這裏吧。

call it a day 是非正式用法。其他例子包括：

After thirty years in politics, I think it's time for me to call it a day.

從政三十年，我想現在也該退休了。

I'm getting a bit tired now — shall we call it a day?

現在我有些累 —— 咱們收工好嗎？

call it a day 的同義詞是 stop。例如：

It is 6 p.m. Let's stopped.

下午六時了，我們收工吧。

It was nearly midnight. Peter decided to stop working.

快將午夜了，彼得決定停止工作。

Try to remember

We'd cleaned half the house and were feeling a bit tired so we decided to call it a day.

我們已清潔半個房間，覺得有點累了，於是就結束了一天的工作。

We called it a day and went home.

我們收工回家。

Other idioms

duty calls，是 "有公務在身" 的意思。例如：

I must go now — duty calls!

我現在要走了 —— 有公務在身。

a close call，是"差點出事，倖免於難"的意思。

　　'That was <u>a close call</u>,' Jacky said, as the boat steadied and got under way.

　　"那真是險象環生，差點出事了。" 當船身穩定，航行正常時，傑克說出這話。

Try the test

□　1. Peter studied hard till 11 p.m. and then decided to call it a night and went to bed.

□　2. Peter studied hard till 11 p.m. and then decided to call it a day and went to bed.

1. ✗　　2. ✓

64   come what may... 不管怎樣……

我們常說"不管發生甚麼情況、不管出現甚麼問題、無論有甚麼困難",
英文是 no matter what happens.。但也可說 Come what may / might /
will...,即"死就死啦、幾大就幾大……"的意思。例如:

Come what may, I'm determined to do it.
不管發生甚麼情況,我已下定決心要這樣做。

She promised to support him come what may.
她答應不管出現甚麼問題都支持他。

I decided that, come what may, the three of us could handle it.
我認定無論發生甚麼事,我們三個人都能應付。

Come what might, he would face the reality and never give up.
無論發生甚麼事,他都會面對現實,絕不放棄。

Try to remember

I'll give you my support. Come what may.
不管發生甚麼情況,我都會支持你。

Come what may, we will never leave Peter.
我們無論如何不會離開彼得。

Come what may... 的同義詞是 No matter what happens...。

Similar idioms

No matter what happens, I will not leave you.
我不管怎樣都不會離開你。

No matter what happens, don't open the door.
不管發生甚麼情況請不要開門。

Try the test

☐   1. Mary has decided to get a university education, come what may.
☐   2. Mary has decided to get a university education, came what might.

1. ✓   2. ✗

65   Crime doesn't pay. 多行不義必自斃。

香港是金錢掛帥、物質主義盛行的社會，罪案有增無減。罪案的英語是 crime，criminal 是 "罪犯" 的意思。例如：

petty / serious crime 是 "輕微 / 嚴重的罪案"，crime prevention 是 "防止罪行"，fight / combat crime 是 "撲滅罪行"，scene of the crime 是 "罪案現場"，to commit a crime 是 "犯罪"。例如：

There has been an increase in violent crime.

暴力犯罪活動一直增加。

Stores spend more and more on crime prevention every year.

商店每年在防止罪案的開支越來越多。

She turned crime when she dropped out of school.

她輟學後淪為罪犯。

The crime rate is rising.

罪案率正在上升。

含 crime 的慣用語有 Crime doesn't pay.，即 "犯罪不划算 / 多行不義必自斃" 的意思。

Try to remember

He has admitted committing several crimes, including two murders.

他承認自己犯過好幾宗案，包括兩宗謀殺案。

The defendant is accused of / charged with a range of crimes.

被告被控一連串罪行。

Try the test

☐   1.   The message you get from the film is simple: crime isn't pay.

☐   2.   The message you get from the film is simple: crime doesn't pay.

1. ✗   2. ✓

66　easier said than done 説得倒容易

表達 "説時容易做時難" 用 easier said than done。例如：

'Why don't you ask Peter to pay?' 'That's <u>easier said than done</u>.'
"你為甚麼不讓彼得付錢？" "説得倒容易。"

We've been told to increase our output, but it's <u>easier said than done</u>.
要求我們增加產量，這可是説來容易做來難了。

Finding the perfect house was <u>easier said than done</u>.
要找到十全十美的房子談何容易。

'All you have to do is ask and get permission from her.' 'Easier said than done — she is in one of her moods today!'
"你不過是要徵求她的同意罷了"。"説容易，今天她又鬧情緒了！"

Try to remember

Avoiding mosquito bites is <u>easier said than done</u>.
要防止蚊子叮咬，説是容易，但很難做到。

I should just tell her to go away, but that's <u>easier said than done</u>.
我應該要她走開，但説容易，做起來困難。

Other idioms

Take it easy.
別急，沉住氣。

Easy come, easy go.
來得容易去得快、易得也易失。

Try the test

☐　1. We talked about reducing our costs, but it is easier said than done.

☐　2. We talked about reducing our costs, but said is easier than done.

1. ✓　　2. ✗

67 fish in troubled waters 渾水摸魚

幾年前香港流行說 "女人是茶煲"，是指女人很麻煩。這個 "茶煲" 來自英文 trouble。它很常用，是 "麻煩、困難" 的意思。例如：

> We have <u>trouble</u> getting good staff.
> 我們在招聘好員工方面有困難。

> The <u>trouble</u> is there aren't any buses at that time.
> 麻煩的是當時沒有公車。

但它也是 "病、痛" 的意思。例如：

> He's been having <u>trouble</u> with his knee.
> 他一直膝痛。

look for trouble 是 "找麻煩、滋事" 的意思；fish in troubled waters 是 "渾水摸魚、趁火打劫" 的意思。例如：

> He started a rumour of a financial crisis so that he could <u>fish in troubled waters</u>.
> 他造謠說有金融危機，以便能渾水摸魚。

Try to remember

> He started a rumour of financial crisis so that he could <u>fish in troubled waters</u>.
> 他造謠說有金融危機，以便能渾水摸魚。

> She's always been good at <u>fishing in troubled waters</u>; she made a lot of money by buying old buildings.
> 她一向很擅長渾水摸魚，她靠買舊建築物發大財。

Other idioms

> <u>Sorry to trouble you</u>, but could you tell me the time?
> 對不起打擾你一下，請問現在幾點鐘？

> If I don't get this finished in time, I'll be <u>in trouble</u>.
> 我如不能及時完成它就有麻煩了。

Try the test

☐ 1. They love to fish in trouble water.

☐ 2. They love to fish in troubled waters.

1. ×   2. ✓

68 Handsome is as / that handsome does.
心美，貌亦美。

我們常說內在美比外在美重要，與 Handsome is as / that handsome does 意思差不多，即"心美，貌亦美"。例如：

> I'm quite pleased with my old car, thank you. Handsome is as handsome does is my motto for cars as well as people.
>
> 我對我的舊車很滿意，謝謝。我的座右銘是心美貌亦美 —— 對人對車都一樣。

它跟 Beauty is but skin-deep. 同義，即"人不可以貌相"。例如：

> Beauty is but skin-deep as they say, but in my opinion, a girl's good qualities are all the more easily appreciated if she is beautiful as well.
>
> 正如人們所說，人不可以貌相。但依我看來，一個素質好的女孩如果長得漂亮，她的品貌就更相得益彰。

Try to remember

> Everyone thinks that Peter is a very handsome boy, but he is very mean too. Handsome is as handsome does.
>
> 人人以為彼得是個很俊美的男孩，可是他很小氣。

My mother always used to say that <u>beauty is only skin-deep</u>.
What is really important is the sort of person you are.

我母親過去常說美貌只是一層皮，重要的是你的為人怎樣。

Other idioms

$1,000 is quite a <u>handsome</u> birthday present.

一千元是很大方的生日禮物。

He said some very <u>handsome</u> things about her.

他替她講了些很友善的話。

Try the test

☐   1. Everyone thinks that Peter is a very handsome boy, but he is very
       mean too. Handsome is as handsome does.

☐   2. Everyone thinks that Peter is a very handsome boy, but he is very
       mean too. Handsome is as handsome is.

1. ✓   2. ✗

69   have a foot in both camps 一腳踏兩船

怎樣可以迅速學會更多詞彙？其中一個方法是把萬用詞典、分類詞彙及各類專科詞典都買下來。當然最有用的是圖解詞典，以 "腳" 為例：

腳踝	ankle
腳後跟	heel
腳背	instep
腳底	sole
腳趾	toes
大腳趾	big toe
尾腳趾	little toe
腳指甲	toenail
腳弓	arch
腳趾球	ball of the foot

再看看 foot：

on your feet	站着
set foot	踏足
have / get cold feet	臨陣畏縮
have a foot in both camps	一腳踏兩船
footage	一段影片 / 片段

Try to remember

The only way to make sure of one's own gain in an argument is to have a foot in both camps.

在辯論中穩操勝券的唯一辦法，就是對不同意見的兩派都支持。

He works in industry and at a university, so he has got a foot in both camps.

他同時在企業和大學裏任職，等於身兼兩職。

Other idioms

Peter is back on his feet again after his operation.

彼得手術後康復了。

The new CEO hopes to get the company <u>back on its feet</u> within six months.

新行政總裁希望六個月內令公司恢復元氣。

Try the test

☐　1. His political opinions aren't very decided or courageous; he keeps feet in both camps.

☐　2. His political opinions aren't very decided or courageous; he keeps a foot in both camps.

1. ✗　2. ✓

70　in the same boat 處境一樣

我們常聽到 "同坐一條船"，那是 in the same boat ，即 "處境一樣、處於相同的困境、面對同樣的危險"。例如：

If you lose your job, I'll lose mine, so we're both <u>in the same boat</u>.

如果你失業，我也會失業，因此我們兩人處境相同。

He's always complaining that he doesn't have enough money, but we're all <u>in the same boat</u>.

他總是抱怨自己錢不夠用，可是我們的處境都一樣。

We're all <u>in the same boat</u>, so let's not criticize each other.

我們大家都同坐一艘船，因此不要互相指責。

> Note：rock the boat 是 "惹麻煩" 的意思。例如：
> Don't <u>rock the boat</u> until negotiations are finished.
> 談判結束之前不要惹麻煩。

Try to remember

We salaried workers are all <u>in the same boat</u> during these hard times.

我們受薪階級在不景氣時都同坐一艘船。

It's no use quarrelling — we are <u>in the same boat</u>.

爭吵沒用，我們同坐一艘船。

Other idioms

The leader of the party asked Peter not to <u>rock the boat</u> until after the election.

黨領導人叫彼得別在選舉前惹麻煩。

They don't like to <u>rock the boat</u> around election time.

他們不喜歡在選舉期間惹麻煩。

Try the test

☐   1. We wage earners are all in a same boat during these hard times.

☐   2. We wage earners are all in the same boat during these hard times.

1. ✗   2. ✓

71　kill two birds with one stone 一舉兩得

學英語成語時，可參考近似的中文成語，例如：

add fuel to the fire / flames	火上加油 / 火上澆油
strike while the iron is hot	打鐵趁熱
fish in troubled waters	渾水摸魚
kill two birds with one stone	一石二鳥 / 一箭雙雕 / 一舉兩得

其他例子包括：

Since Susan and Peter live near my parents, I'll call in on them as well and kill two birds with one stone.

既然蘇珊和彼得都住我父母家附近，我就順便探望他們，一舉兩得。

I killed two birds with one stone and picked the kids up on the way to the station.

我在去車站的路上順便接了孩子，真是一舉兩得。

Try to remember

The teacher told us that making an outline kills two birds with one stone.

老師告訴我們撰寫大綱是一石二鳥。

Peter killed two birds with one stone, both shopping and looking for a shop of his own to rent.

彼得一舉兩得，即購了物又找了自己要租的商店。

Other idioms

Having a baby can be kill or cure for a troubled marriage.

要小孩對陷入感情困境的婚姻可謂是孤注一擲。

The plane was late, so I killed two hours window-shopping.

飛機晚點了，我在商店裏逛了兩個小時打發時間。

Try the test

- ☐ 1. He wished to kill all his birds with one stone.
- ☐ 2. He wished to kill all his birds with stones.

1. ✓   2. ✗

72   more haste, less speed 欲速則不達

表示 "匆忙、倉促、匆促"，英語是 haste。例如：

She packed her bags <u>in haste</u> when she heard the police were looking for her.

她聽見警察到處尋找自己時，就匆忙收拾行裝。

<u>In her haste</u>, she forgot to take her umbrella.

匆忙之中她忘了帶雨傘。

<u>In his haste</u> to complete on time, she made a number of mistakes.

匆忙之中他想按時完成，結果出了不少錯。

More haste, less speed 是 "欲速則不達" 的意思，它是慣用語，也作 the more haste, the less speed。例如：

Tell me the story from the beginning. And take time. <u>More haste, less speed</u>, you know.

從頭開始將這個故事告訴我，慢慢來。欲速則不達，你是知道的。

more haste, less speed 的同義詞是 haste makes waste。

Try to remember

<u>Make haste, less speed</u>. Please do it slowly and carefully.

欲速則不達，請慢慢小心做。

If you do it too quickly, you are likely to make mistakes. Haste makes waste.

如果你做得太快，大有可能出錯，欲速則不達。

Other idioms

In haste, she forgot to lock the door.

匆忙之中她忘記鎖門。

In her haste to get up from the table, she knocked over a glass.

她匆忙從桌邊站起來，結果碰翻了一隻玻璃杯。

Try the test

☐   1. Bring the doctor with more haste.

☐   2. Bring the doctor in haste.

1. ✗   2. ✓

73 not my cup of tea 非某人所好

很多人常說 "這不是我杯茶"，是 not my cup of tea 的直譯，表示某事不合乎某人心意或不合乎某人喜好，常與否定詞連用。例如：

He invited me to the opera but it is really <u>not my cup of tea</u>.

他邀請我看歌劇，其實我並不喜歡。

Surely I'll go swimming with you. That is just <u>my cup of tea</u>.

我肯定會跟你一起游泳，這正是我喜歡的。

Game shows just <u>aren't my cup of tea</u>.

我對有獎競賽節目不感興趣。

Playing cards <u>isn't my cup of tea</u>. Let's watch television instead.

我不喜歡打牌，我們看電視吧。

> Note：cup 與 mug 不同。mug 是帶柄大杯 / 大玻璃杯。

Try to remember

Thanks for inviting me, but hockey <u>isn't my cup of tea</u>.

謝謝你邀請我，不過我不大喜歡看曲棍球。

She is nice enough but <u>not really my cup of tea</u>.

她這人挺不錯，但不是我特別喜歡的那種人。

Other idioms

I <u>like</u> that cup and saucer.

我喜歡那套杯碟。

She held the sweets <u>in the cup of her hand</u>.

她把糖果捧在手心。

Try the test

☐ 1. Long walks are not my tea of cup.

☐ 2. Long walks are not my cup of tea.

1. ✗   2. ✓

74   on the spur of the moment 一時衝動

我們常說 "一時衝動"，英語是 on the spur of the moment，即 "心血來潮、一時興致" 的意思。例如：

I phoned her up <u>on the spur of the moment</u>.

我一時心血來潮打了電話給她。

He admitted he had taken the vehicle <u>on the spur of the moment</u>.

他承認自己因一時衝動擅自取去那輛車。

When they called me with the offer of a job in Japan, I decided <u>on the spur of the moment to accept</u>.

他們打電話給我，提供一份在日本的工作，我一時衝動就答應下來。

Spur-of-the-moment 是非正式用語，只放在名詞前面修飾名詞。例如：

We hadn't planned to go away — it was one of those <u>spur-of-the-moment</u> decisions.

我們沒有計劃要離開 —— 這是一時衝動作出的決定。

Try to remember

He jumped in a car <u>on the spur of the moment</u> and drove to the peak.

他一時心血來潮，跳上車並駛往山頂。

She stole the money <u>on the spur of the moment</u>.

她一時衝動才偷了那些錢。

Other idioms

Ambition <u>spurred her on</u>.

野心促使她付出更大努力。

Peter <u>was spurred on</u> by his desire to do better than the other boys.

彼得付出更大努力，因他渴望比其他男孩優勝。

Try the test

☐ 1. We decided to go to China on the spur of a moment.

☐ 2. We decided to go to China on the spur of the moment.

1. ✗   2. ✓

75 out of the question 絕不可能

我們常説 "問題"，英語是 question。例如：

> In the examination, there is sure to be a <u>question</u> on pollution.
>
> 考試時一定有關於污染的問題。

> The <u>question</u> is, how much are you going to pay them?
>
> 問題是你打算給他們多少錢。

beyond question 是 "毋庸置疑" 的意思。例如：

> Her honesty is <u>beyond question</u>.
>
> 她的誠實是毋庸置疑的。

open to question 是 "還需要考慮" 的意思。例如：

> His suitability for the job is <u>open to question</u>.
>
> 他是否適合擔任這份工作還需要考慮。

out of the question 是 "不可能、絕不可能" 的意思。例如：

> Another trip abroad this year is <u>out of the question</u>.
>
> 今年再度出國是絕不可能的。

> Note：out of question 是 "沒問題" 的意思。

Try to remember

A loan of $100,000 is <u>out of the question</u>.

貸款十萬元是不可能的了。

Taking another holiday is <u>out of the question</u>.

再放假是不可能的了。

out of the question 的同義詞是 There is no question.

Other idioms

There is <u>no question of</u> agreeing to the demands.

同意這些要求是不可能的。

There is <u>no question of</u> us interfering in the running of the business.

我們決不會插手公司的經營。

Try the test

☐   1. As for going back — that is quite out of the question.

☐   2. As for going back — that is quite out of questions.

1. ✓   2. ✗

76   packed like sardines 擠迫不堪

香港人對繁忙時間 rush hour, the morning / evening rush hour 或高峰時間 peak hours 應該印象深刻。例如：

> The roads are full of traffic <u>at peak hours</u>.
> 在高峰時間馬路上交通十分繁忙。

> Don't travel <u>at rush hour / in the rush hour</u>.
> 別在繁忙時間乘車。

pack 也可以用作動詞，描述擠迫的情況。例如：

> The streets <u>were packed with</u> men, women and children.
> 街上擠滿了男男女女和小孩子。

"擠得水洩不通"，非正式英語是 pack / cram / squash like sardines。例如：

> We <u>were packed like sardines</u> on the train.
> 我們在火車裏擠得像（罐頭裏的）沙甸魚。

> Note："非繁忙時間" 是 off-peak hours。

Try to remember

> We were <u>squashed like sardines</u> in the rush-hour bus.
> 我們像沙甸魚一樣擠在繁忙時間的公車上。

> Economy class passengers <u>were packed in</u> like sardines.
> 經濟艙的乘客擠得像沙甸魚一樣。

Other idioms

> Fans <u>packed</u> the stadium to watch the match.
> 球迷湧進體育館觀看比賽。

> The MTR was so <u>packed</u> that I couldn't find a seat in the car.
> 港鐵擠滿了人，我在車廂內一個座位也找不到。

Try the test

☐　1. We were packed like sardine fish in the train to Fanling.

☐　2. We were packed like sardines in the train to Fanling.

1. ✗   2. ✓

77   Practice makes perfect. 熟能生巧。

要學好英文寫作，必須勤加練習，所謂熟能生巧，只要不荒廢、不生疏，英文就會寫得好。起步階段時，寫簡單的段落是很好的做法，一段約 60 個字，並且只用一種時態，配合常用詞語、簡單句和複合句，就不會有很大困難。找人批改是一個問題，但只要我們一段用一個主題句 topic sentence，比如寫給普通朋友討論和尋求意見，不會有很大困難。

Try to remember

I often write because I believe practice makes perfect.
我常常寫作，因我相信熟能生巧。

Practice makes perfect.   That's why she practices the violin for long hours.
熟能生巧，因此她長時間練習小提琴。

Other idioms

Bribery is a common practice in many countries.
賄賂在許多國家都司空見慣。

We urge you to put the committee's recommendations into practice.
我們敦促你把委員會的建議付諸實行。

Try the test

☐   1. A delightful theory! I must put into practice.

☐   2. A delightful theory! I must put it into practice.

1. ✗   2. ✓

78 red-handed 當場

red 是 "紅色" 的意思，它是形容詞。例如：

> Her eyes were <u>red</u> from crying.
>
> 她眼睛都哭紅了。

它也是名詞。例如：

> She often wears <u>red</u>.
>
> 她經常穿紅色衣服。

含紅色的常用詞組包括：

red blood cell	紅血球
red card	紅牌
red tape	繁文縟節
red carpet	紅地氈

go through / run a red light 是 "衝紅燈"，等於 jump / run the lights。

red-handed 是 "當場" 的意思。例如：

> They caught him <u>red-handed</u> when he was just putting the diamonds in his pocket.
>
> 他正要把鑽石放進口袋時，他們當場把他抓住了。

> Note：be in the red 是 "負債、虧損" 的意思。例如：
> The company has plunged $50 million <u>into the red</u>.
> 公司負債已達 5,000 萬元。

Try to remember

> He was caught <u>red-handed</u> when he was cheating in the exam.
>
> 他正在考試作弊時當場被抓住了。

> They caught the man <u>red-handed</u> in the robbery.
>
> 他在搶劫時，被他們當場抓住了。

red-handed 的同義詞是 on the spot。

Other idioms

You can be sacked <u>on the spot</u> for stealing.

偷竊會被當場開除的。

We'll give him the <u>red-carpet</u> treatment.

我們將會舉行隆重儀式歡迎他。

Try the test

☐　1.　A man was caught red-handed in the robbery.

☐　2.　A man caught red-handed in the robbery.

1. ✓　2. ✗

79　so far, so good 一切還算順利

我們常描述自己對目前環境或狀況的感想，so far, so good 是 "到目前為止，一切還算順利" 的意思。例如：

We're over the wall. <u>So far, so good</u>. Now we've got to swim the river.

我們已越過了牆，一切還算順利。現在我們必須游過河去。

I've found a tin of beans. <u>So far, so good</u>, but where is the opener?

我找到一罐豆，到目前為止，一切還不錯。但開罐器在哪裏呢？

<u>So far, so good</u> — about 95 per cent of calls have been answered within five seconds.

到目前為止，一切順利。大約95%的電話在5秒鐘內都有人接聽。

'How's your new job?' 'So far so good.'

"你的新工作怎麼樣？" "到目前為止，一切都好。"

Try to remember

So far, so good, I hope we keep on with such good luck.

目前為止，一切順利。我希望能保持好運氣。

I was worried that my math course was going to be difficult, but so far, so good.

原擔心我的數學課程會很難，但到目前為止，一切尚好。

Other idioms

The present economic situation is a far cry from the one predicted.

目前的經濟情況遠不如之前預料的。

The court ruled that the police went too far when they handcuffed Peter to a chair.

法庭裁定，警察把彼得拷到椅上的做法太過份。

Try the test

☐   1. So far, so good; I hope we keep on with such good luck.

☐   2. So far, so well; I hope we keep on with such good luck.

1. ✓   2. ✗

80   slap in the face 侮辱

我們常説"侮辱、打擊",除了 insult 和 blow 外,還可説 slap in the face,它是非正式用語。例如:

It was a slap in the face for his parents when he ignored their advice and gave up his job.

他無視父母的忠告,放棄了自己的工作。這無疑對他父母是個打擊。

It was a real slap in the face for her when he refused to go out to dinner with her.

他拒絕和她一起出去吃晚飯,這對她真是一種侮辱。

> Note: a slap on the wrist 是"輕微的懲罰、溫和的警告"的意思。例如:
> The law ought to be tougher, we shouldn't just give criminals a slap on the wrist!
> 法律應當更嚴厲,我們不應對犯罪分子判處輕微的懲罰!

Try to remember

It was a slap in the face when the bank turned him down.

銀行拒絕貸款給他,對他真是個打擊。

I worked hard on the paper, so it was a slap in the face to get a bad grade.

我辛辛苦苦寫出這篇論文,得分很低對我是個打擊。

Other idioms

The judge gave Susan a slap on the wrist for not wearing her seat belt.

法官因為蘇珊沒有繫安全帶而對她稍稍懲戒了一下。

She slapped him across his face.

她抽了他一記耳光。

Try the test

☐   1. Peter slapped our club in face by saying that everyone in it was stupid.

☐   2. Peter slapped our club in the face by saying that everyone in it was stupid.

1. ✗   2. ✓

81   speak of the devil 說曹操，曹操就到

在日常生活，我們常說"說曹操，曹操就到"，英語是 speak / talk of the devil。它是非正式說法。例如：

'Peter hasn't been here for some time. Wonder what's up with him.'

"彼得有相當長的時間沒來這裏。不知他怎樣。"

'Speak of the devil! Here he comes now.'

"說曹操，曹操就到！他剛來了。"

'I haven't seen Susan for a while.' 'Well speak of the devil, here she is!'

"我有一陣子沒見蘇珊了""真是說曹操，曹操就到！她來了。"

也可說 speak of the devil and he appears (will appear)。例如：

We were just talking about Peter when he came in the door. Speak of the devil and he appears.

他們正談論彼得時，他就進了門。真是說到他，他就到。

Try to remember

Did you hear what happened to Susan yesterday — oh, speak of the devil, here she is.

你聽説昨天發生在蘇珊身上的那件事了嗎 —— 噢，説曹操，曹操就到了。

Talk of the devil — here's Peter now!

噢，説曹操，曹操就到 —— 看，彼得出現在眼前了。

Other idioms

He's been ill for weeks, poor devil.

他已病了好幾個星期了，可憐的傢伙。

I hear you've got a new car, you lucky devil!

我聽説你得到了一輛新車，你這個幸運兒。

Try the test

☐　1.　She has lost her job, a poor devil.

☐　2.　She has lost her job, poor devil.

1. ✗　　2. ✓

82   stab someone in the back 陷害

stab 是 "我們用刀等銳器刺、戳、捅" 的意思。例如：

She was <u>stabbed to death</u> in the attack.

她遭到襲擊，被刺死了。

He <u>stabbed her in the arm</u> with a screwdriver.

他用螺絲刀在她的胳膊上戳了一下。

我們常說 "插、戳背脊、戳人家背部"，就是 stab someone in the back，即 "陷害、中傷、背後中傷某人" 的意思。例如：

Susan promised to support me at the meeting, but then she <u>stabbed me in the back</u> by supporting Peter instead.

蘇珊最初答應在會上支持我，可是最後她反過來支持彼得，在我背後捅了一刀。

> Note：stab 也是名詞。例如：
> She received several <u>stabs</u> in the chest.
> 她胸部被刺了幾刀。

Try to remember

She had been lied to and <u>stabbed in the back</u> by people that she thought were her friends.

她曾被一些自己視為朋友的人欺騙過，在背後被捅過刀子。

You <u>stabbed him in the back</u> when you smiled and laughed with him , and then told everyone not to go to his party.

你當面對着他有講有笑，然後告訴大家不要出席他的聚會，你是在背後傷害他。

stab someone in the back 的同義詞是 betray。

Other idioms

He felt betrayed by his father's <u>lack of support</u>.

他覺得父親背棄了他，因為父親沒有支持他。

She was offered money to betray her colleagues.
有人收買她，要她出賣自己的同事。

Try the test

☐   1. Could young Mary really have betrayed the tradition?

☐   2. Was young Mary really betrayed the tradition?

1. ✓   2. ✗

83   stand on your own feet 自食其力

一些青少年在成長期內不喜歡跟父母生活，有些總是希望離開父母獨立生活，自食其力，英語是 stand on your own (two) feet。 它是非正式用語。例如：

When his parents died he had to learn to stand on his own (two) feet.
他父母去世後，他不得不學會自立。

She'll have to get a job and learn to stand on her own two feet sooner and later.
她遲早要找份工作，學會自食其力。

Try to remember

Early poverty had taught Peter to stand on his own feet.
年輕時貧窮的生活令彼得學會自食其力。

Susan offered to help me, but I told her I would rather stand on my own feet.
蘇珊建議幫我，但我對她説我寧可自食其力。

Other idioms

standing on your head 與 "自食其力" 無關，它也是非正式用語，是 "輕而易舉、易如反掌" 的意思。例如：

It's the sort of program Peter could write <u>standing on his head</u>.

寫這種程式對彼得來説易如反掌。

A genius like you can solve that problem <u>standing on your head</u>!

像你這樣的天才，可以毫不費力解決那個問題！

stand on ceremony 是 "講究禮節、拘禮" 的意思。例如：

Please sit down and make yourself comfortable, we don't <u>stand on ceremony</u> here.

請坐，隨便一點，我們這裏不必拘禮。

Do take your jacket off; we don't <u>stand on ceremony</u> in this house.

脱下你的夾克吧，我們家裏不拘泥於禮節。

stand back 等於 step backwards，是 "向後站" 的意思；Stand clear of the train doors, please. 則是 "請勿站近車門。" 的意思。

Try the test

☐   1. My uncle offered to help me, but I told him I would rather stand on my own foot.

☐   2. My uncle offered to help me, but I told him I would rather stand on my own feet.

1. ✗   2. ✓

84   strike while the iron's hot 打鐵趁熱

生活在節奏緊迫、競爭劇烈的香港，很多人都知道做任何事都必須夠快，hurry up, in a hurry。例如：

Hurry up! We're going to be late.

快點！我們要遲到了。

He had to leave in a hurry.

他不得不趕快離開。

我們也說 "打鐵趁熱、捷足先登"。剛好英文也有類似成語。例如：

They don't often make such offers — I'd strike while the iron's hot if I were you.

他們不常主動提出這樣的建議 —— 我要是你的話就趁熱打鐵，趕快答應。

The early bird catches the worm.

捷足先登。

Make hay while the sun shines.

勿失良機。

Try to remember

Dad is happy and relaxed and just got paid; let's strike while the iron is hot and ask if we can use the car.

父親心情輕鬆愉快，又剛發工資，咱們趁熱打鐵，問他我們可否借用他的車。

To overtake the enemy, we must strike the iron while it is hot.

為了超過敵人，我們必須趁熱打鐵。

strike while the iron's hot 的同義是 make hay while the sun shines。

Other idioms

She advised him to make hay while the sun shines.

她勸他勿失良機。

Let's set out at dawn, you know, <u>the early bird catches the worm</u>.

咱們晨曦出發，這叫捷足先登。

Try the test

☐   1. This is a good job. Make hay while the sun shines.

☐   2. This is a good job. Make hay when the sun shines.

1. ✓   2. ✗

85   take it or leave it 要不要隨你

學英語時應選一些簡單實用，但搭配豐富的詞彙，如 take。例如：

Take it or leave it.

要不要隨你 / 接不接受由你。

I'll give you $100 — <u>take it or leave it</u>.

我會給你 100 元 —— 要不要隨你。

That's my final offer — you can <u>take it or leave it</u>.

那是我最後的報價了 —— 接不接受隨你。

take your time 是 "不要急，慢慢來" 的意思。例如：

The decorators are really <u>taking their time</u>.

那些裝修工人真的會慢慢來。

not take long 是 "不久"。例如：

I'm just going to the shops. I <u>won't take long</u>.

我只是去商店買點東西，不會去太久。

Try to remember

He said the price of the house is $1 million, <u>take it or leave it</u>.

他說房子的價錢是一百萬元，要不要隨你的便。

$10,000 is the price. Take it or leave it.

價錢是一萬元，要不要隨你的便。

Other idioms

I need a shower — I won't take long.

我要洗個澡，不會太久。

It'll take time for him to recover from the illness.

他的病需要很長時間才能康復。

Try the test

☐　1. Do you like sugar in your tea? — I don't mind. I can take or leave it.

☐　2. Do you like sugar in your tea? — I don't mind. I can take it or leave it.

1. ✗　　2. ✓

86   the more the merrier 多多益善

作文時常要作出比較，如 the more, less , etc..., the more, less, etc... 即 "越……越……"，例如：

> The more he thought about it, the more depressed he became.
>
> 這件事他越想越感到沮喪。

> The less said about the whole thing, the happier they'll be.
>
> 對這整件事情談得越少，他們越高興。

> The more I see of him, the less I like him.
>
> 我越是多看見他，越是不喜歡他。

> The more she eats, the fatter she gets.
>
> 她越吃越胖。

英語成語中有 The more the merrier 即 "人越多越熱鬧、（東西）多多益善、越多越好的意思"。例如：

> 'Can I bring a friend to your party?' 'Sure — the more the merrier!'
>
> "我能帶個朋友來你的聚會嗎？" "當然可以。人越多越熱鬧嘛！"

Try to remember

> The more he drank, the more violent he became.
>
> 酒他喝得越多，就越變得暴躁。

> The more he insisted he was innocent, the less they seemed to believe him.
>
> 他越堅持自己無辜，他們似乎越不相信他。

Other idioms

> Do you mind if I bring a couple of friends to your party? Not at all — the more the merrier!
>
> 你不介意我帶幾個朋友參加你的聚會吧？一點也不介意，人越多越高興。

> The more who come to the party, the more fun we'll have, or as

they say, <u>the more, the merrier</u>.

參加聚會的人越多越好玩，或者正如他們說人越多越開心。

Try the test

☐ 1. The more angry she became, the more she laughed at him.

☐ 2. The more angry she became, she laughed at him the more.

1. ✓   2. ✗

87   There is no smoke without fire.

無風不起浪。

有時候某人或某事物面對一些不利的批評，背後也許會有理由。英語裏的成語 There is no smoke without fire. 就是這個意思，美式英語是 Where there's smoke, there's fire.。它是口語，即 "無風不起浪" 或 "空穴來風，事必有因" 的意思。例如：

He said the accusations are not true, but <u>there's no smoke without fire</u>.

他說那些指責毫無根據，但無風不起浪。

He considered that Susan had behaved badly. He constantly repeated the old adage, that <u>there was no smoke without fire</u>.

他認為蘇珊行為不端正。他總反覆講到 "無風不起浪" 這句古諺。

Note：second-hand smoke 是 "二手煙"。

Try to remember

Why was he fired? I don't know, but there is no smoke without fire.

為何他被開除我不知道，但空穴來風，事必有因。

Although he had been found not guilty in court, people are saying that there's no smoke without fire.

儘管法庭宣判他無罪，但人們還在說無風不起浪。

Other idioms

Without a scholarship, her dreams of university would go up in smoke.

沒有獎學金，她上大學的夢想就成為泡影。

The whole house went up in smoke.

整座房屋被燒毀了。

Try the test

☐ 1. All her plans have gone up with smoke.

☐ 2. All her plans have gone up in smoke.

1. ✗   2. ✓

88   Those were the days. 那些日子真好。

大家也許聽過由 Mary Hopkins 主唱的一首膾炙人口的歌，歌名是 *Those were the days, my friends*。以下節錄其中一段歌詞：

Those were the days, my friend

We thought they'd never end

We'd sing and dance forever and a day

We'd live the life we choose

We'd fight and never lose

For we were young and sure to have our way

La la la la la la

La la la la la la

歌詞裏面 Those were the days，意思是 "那些日子真好，那才是好時光"，以下還有其他例句：

We used to stay in bed all morning and party all night. Those were the days!

我們以前常常睡整個上午也不起牀，還通宵開派對。那些日子真好！

They bought the house for $10,000 in 1972. Ah, those were the days!

他們在 1972 年花 10,000 元買下這房子。哦，那才是好時光呢！

I can remember when we could buy a cinema ticket and a big bag of popcorn and still have a change from ten dollars. Ah, those were the days!

我記得那時我們用十元買了張電影票和一大包爆谷，還剩下幾塊錢，哦，那才是好時光呢！

Try to remember

We were young and madly in love. Ah, those were the days!

我們當時都年輕，正處於熱戀之中。哦，那時候多好啊！

Do you remember when we first got married? Those were the days!

你還記得我們剛結婚那時嗎？那時多幸福！

Other idioms

<u>In those days</u>, people used to write a lot more letters.

過去人們寫信要多得多。

Didn't I see you in the bank <u>the other day</u>?

前幾天，我不是在銀行見過你嗎？

Try the test

☐   1. On those days, she used to help her mother with her cooking.

☐   2. In those days, she used to help her mother with her cooking.

1. ✗   2. ✓

89 表達"所以"不一定用 therefore

作文常用"因此、所以",特別常用於句首。英語除了 therefore、thus 和 hence,可以説 accordingly。例如:

> The cost of raw materials rose sharply last year. Accordingly, we were forced to increase our prices.
>
> 去年原材料成本大幅度提高,因此我們被迫加價。

> Some of the laws were contradictory. Accordingly, measures were taken to clarify them.
>
> 有些法例互相矛盾,因此已採取措施澄清。

它也是"照着、相應地"的意思。例如:

> We have to discover their plans and act accordingly.
>
> 我們要找出他們的計劃照着辦。

> Susan still considered her a child and treated her accordingly.
>
> 蘇珊仍把她當小孩一樣看待。

Try to remember

> There aren't many jobs available. Accordingly, companies receive hundreds of resumes for every opening.
>
> 就業職位不多,因此每個空缺公司都收到數以百計的履歷。

> He is an expert in his field, and is paid accordingly.
>
> 他是這個領域的專家,並得到了相應報酬。

Other examples

> He's only 16 and therefore not eligible to vote.
>
> 他只有 16 歲,因此沒有投票選舉的資格。

There is still much to discuss. We shall, <u>therefore</u>, return to this item at our next meeting.

要討論的問題還有很多，所以我們將在下次會議上再討論這項議題。

Try the test

☐   1. He told me to lock the door and I acted according to him.

☐   2. He told me to lock the door and I acted accordingly.

1. ✗   2. ✓

90   affair 有多種用法

affair 很常用，解作 "公共 / 政治活動 / 私人業務"，屬於複數。current affairs 是 "時事"，world / international / business / foreign affairs 是 "世界 / 國際 / 商業 / 外交事務"，例如：

He looked after his father's <u>financial affairs</u>.

他管理父親的財務。

解作 "曖昧關係、有染" 時，它是可數名詞。例如：

She is having <u>an affair</u> with her boss.

她跟老闆有染。

但解作 "個人的事" 時，卻是單數。例如：

How I spend my money is <u>my affair</u>.

我怎樣用錢是我自己的事。

同樣，它作為 "事件" 的意思時也通常是單數。例如：

The newspapers exaggerated the whole <u>affair</u>.

報章誇大了整件事。

Try to remember

She is having an affair with a married man.

她和一個有婦之夫私通。

He organized his financial affairs very efficiently.

他把自己的財務處理得井井有條。

Other examples

Peter said his planned 5-day visit would be a purely private affair.

彼得説他計劃的五天訪問純屬私事。

He does not want to interfere in the internal affairs of another country.

他不想干涉別國內政。

Try the test

☐   1. Leave me alone, mind your own affairs.

☐   2. Leave me alone, mind your affair.

1. ✓   2. ✗

91 "每隔……分鐘" 英文該怎說？

表達每隔一段時間或距離用 at intervals，如在長跑比賽裏，跑手每隔兩分鐘分批出發，The runners started at 2-minute intervals.。其他例子包括：

Buses to Yuen Long leave at regular intervals.

到元朗的公共汽車按既定時段開出。

We see each other at regular intervals — about once a month.

我們每隔一段時間見面 —— 大約一個月一次。

In the event of fire, the alarm will sound at 15-second intervals / at intervals of 15 seconds.

發生火警時，警鐘每隔 15 秒就會響一次。

Flaming torches were positioned at intervals along the road.

沿馬路每隔一段距離插着燃燒着的火炬。

Try to remember

There is an interval of a week between Christmas and New Year's Day.

聖誕節和新年相隔一個星期。

I always get hungry in the interval between breakfast and lunch.

我總是在早餐和午餐之間感到肚子餓。

Other examples

We stopped at 110 kilometres intervals to use the toilet.

我們每行駛 110 公里停下來上廁所。

There was a long interval of silence.

出現了長時間的沉默。

Try the test

☐　1.　She bought us coffee at interval.

☐　2.　She bought us coffee at intervals.

1. ✗　2. ✓

92　大人物和"槍"、"車輪" 有關嗎？

很多人都知道 small 和 big 的意思。請看以下含 big 的詞組：

a big man / house / increase	高大的男人 / 大房子 / 大幅度增加
a big eater / drinker / spender	飯量大的人 / 酒量大的人 / 大豪客
a big name / big gun / big shot / big wheel	大人物 / 知名人士 / 重要人物
big money	賺大錢
a big blow	令人晴天霹靂的事
full of big ideas	形容某人雄心勃勃
a big mouth	多嘴 / 吹牛
a big head	自高自大的人

Note："高大威猛的男孩" 是 big boy，不是 large boy。large boy 是 "大塊頭"。

Try to remember

He's a big gun in politics.

他是政界要人。

She's a big shot in advertising.

她是廣告界翹楚。

Other examples

'I ran five miles this morning.' 'No big deal! I ran ten.'

"今早我跑了 5 英哩。" "沒甚麼了不起，我跑了 10 英哩。"

We'll have to pay a little more — it's no big deal.

我們將不得不多付一些錢 —— 這沒甚麼大不了。

Try the test

☐　1.　Susan had been a big shot in secondary school.

☐　2.　Susan had been a large shot in secondary school.

1. ✓　2. ✗

93 如何用 blunt 形容人

要表達剪刀和鉛筆很鋒利、很尖，英語是 sharp。例如：a <u>sharp</u> knife / <u>sharp</u> teeth，I cut my foot on a <u>sharp</u> stone。若想表達刀很鈍，該怎說呢？

其實我們查一查英漢詞典，就會找到 blunt，也可以查漢英詞典，但必須用英語詞典學會 blunt。例如：

It is a <u>blunt</u> knife.

這刀很鈍。

My pencil's <u>blunt</u> — can I borrow your sharpener?

我的鉛筆鈍了，能借用你的削筆刀嗎？

> Note：它也是 "說話粗魯、不客氣" 的意思。例如：
> He is a <u>blunt</u> man.
> 他是個說話粗魯的人。
> To be <u>blunt</u> / To put it <u>bluntly</u>, his work is appalling.
> 不客氣的說，他做得很糟糕。

Try to remember

He is holding a knife with a <u>blunt</u> edge.

他正手持一把刀刃不鋒利的刀。

The victim was hit on the head with a <u>blunt</u> object.

受害人被鈍器擊中頭部。

Other examples

She told me <u>bluntly</u> that I should lose weight.

她直言不諱地告訴我，我應該減肥。

To put it bluntly, I can't afford it.

坦率地說，我買不起。

Try the test

☐ 1. Let's blunt, young people will not buy this car.

☐ 2. Let's be blunt, young people will not buy this car.

1. ✗   2. ✓

94 "感到極無聊"英文該怎說？

日常生活裏少不免對人或事物感到"厭倦、煩悶"，最簡單的是 bored。
它是形容詞。例如：

> The children quickly got bored with staying indoors.
> 孩子們在屋裏很快悶得發慌了。

> There was a bored expression on his face.
> 他臉上有種厭倦的表情。

boring 是"事物令人厭倦"的意思。例如：

> He's such a boring man!
> 他就是這麼一個惹人厭倦的人。

> It is a boring job / book / evening.
> 這是無聊的工作 / 書 / 夜晚。

> Susan found her job very boring.
> 蘇珊覺得自己的工作很無聊。

> Note：bored stiff / bored to death / tears / bored out of your mind 是"厭煩透了、
> 極其厭倦、無聊透頂"的意思。

boredom 是名詞，例如：

> In many cases, boredom in class causes children to be
> disruptive.
> 在許多情況下，課堂沉悶導致孩子變得愛搗蛋。

> To relieve the boredom in the traffic jam, Lisa listened to her
> favourite songs.
> 為減少塞車引起的沉悶，麗莎聆聽她最喜歡的歌曲。

此外，bore 也可以用作名詞，例如：

> His wife is such a bore.
> 他太太真令人厭煩。

> Jenny found doing housework a real bore.
> 珍妮發覺做家務實在令人厭煩。

Try to remember

He didn't enjoy the lesson and he <u>was bored</u>.

他不喜歡這課，感到很悶。

The lesson was long and <u>boring</u>.

這課長而且沉悶。

Other examples

It is <u>boring</u> to sit on the plane with nothing to read.

坐在飛機上沒東西可讀真無聊。

He <u>was getting bored with / of</u> doing the same thing every day.

每天都做同樣的事，他感到很無聊。

Try the test

☐   1. I was bored to die before the first was out.

☐   2. I was bored to death before the first was out.

1. ✗   2. ✓

95 含 break 的常用語和短語動詞

break 有很多常用片語和短語動詞。例如：

break the ice	聚會開始時，用言語或行動打破隔閡
break into pieces	打碎
break down	失聲痛哭
break up	情侶分手
break through	突破

Try to remember

The fire must have broken out during the night.

這場火肯定是在夜間燒起來的。

The two countries have broken off diplomatic relations.

這兩個國家已斷絕了外交關係。

Other examples

I had a breakdown in the middle of the road.

我的汽車在半路上拋錨了。

Both sides blamed each other for the breakdown of talks.

雙方都指責對方導致了談判的破裂。

Try the test

☐ 1. His health broke down.

☐ 2. His health was broken down.

1. ✓　2. ✗

96   量詞如串 / 束 / 群可用 bunch 表達

要形容或描述一些物件或東西的數量，除了使用數詞，如阿拉伯數字，或 hundred, thousand, million 和 billion 之外，還可以配合適當的量詞造句。例如：

bunch	一串 / 一束 / 一紮
a bunch of bananas / grapes	一把香蕉 / 一串葡萄
a bunch of keys	一串鑰匙

He picked me a bunch of flowers.
他給我採了一束鮮花。

它也是 "大量、大批、一群" 的意思，特別是美式英語，它是非正式用語。例如：

I have a whole bunch of stuff to do this evening.
我今天傍晚有一大堆工作。

A bunch of girls was / were sitting on the grass.
一群女孩坐在草地上。

Try to remember

My neighbours are a bunch of busybodies.
我鄰居是一群愛管閒事的人。

We did a bunch of songs together.
我們一起唱了許多歌。

Other examples

They are a lovely bunch who have made me feel welcome.
他們這群人真可愛，讓我感到賓至如歸。

They bought a bunch of things at the store.
他們在商店裏買了一大堆東西。

Try the test

☐   1. A bunch of grape hung from the vine.

☐   2. A bunch of grapes hung from the vine.

1. ✗   2. ✓

97 "忍不住" 英文該怎說 ?

我們常說 "不禁、忍不住（或無法抑制）做某事、不可能避免某事"，英語是 can't help。例如：

He <u>can't help</u> thinking she knows more than she has told him.
他不禁覺得她沒把知道的全部告訴他。

She always ends up having an argument with him, she doesn't know why, she just <u>can't help</u> it.
她總是和他意見不合，鬧得不歡而散。她不知道為甚麼，她就是忍不住。

I <u>couldn't help</u> it if the train was late.
火車晚點了，我也沒辦法。

He burst out laughing — he <u>couldn't help</u> himself.
他突然大笑起來 —— 他控制不住自己。

She <u>can't help</u> herself, she doesn't mean to be so rude.
她控制不了自己，她並不想那麼無禮。

Try to remember

I know I shouldn't eat so much chocolate, but I <u>can't help</u> myself.
我知道我不該吃太多巧克力，只是我無法控制自己。

It was awful, but I <u>couldn't help</u> laughing.
這真糟糕，可我還是忍不住大笑起來。

Other examples

'Stop giggling!' 'I can't help it.'
"別再笑了！""我忍不住呀。"

I shouldn't have said it but I <u>couldn't help</u> myself.
我當時不應該說，但我實在忍不住。

Try the test

☐　1. I couldn't help it. It was an impulse.

☐　2. I couldn't help. It was an impulse.

1. ✓　2. ✗

98 "軟硬兼施"英文該怎説？

有些老師喜歡在課堂上以"軟硬兼施、威逼利誘"的態度對待學生，英語是 carrot and stick 或 the stick and the carrot。例如：

> I believe in <u>using the carrot instead of the stick</u> in the classroom.
> 課堂上我贊成用軟不用硬。

> Their method of negotiation is <u>a combination of the carrot and the stick</u>.
> 他們談判的方法就是威逼利誘。

> Last month, a federal commission proposed <u>a carrot-and-stick approach</u> to punish and deter corporate crime.
> 上月，一個聯邦委員會提出一項恩威並重的方法來懲罰和遏制公司罪行。

Try to remember

> Peter's mother used the <u>carrot and stick</u> when she talked about his low grades.
> 彼得的母親談到他差勁的成績時，用了好則獎勵壞則懲罰的方法。

> Bill is using <u>the carrot-and-stick approach</u> to the problem.
> 比爾正在用軟硬兼施辦法處理問題。

Other examples

> My father believed in <u>the carrot-and-stick approach</u> with us, but the carrots were pretty scarce.
> 我父親相信軟硬兼施對我們有效，然而獎勵少得可憐。

> The <u>carrot-and-stick theory</u> of motivation work reasonably well under certain circumstances.
> 威逼利誘的激勵理論在一定情況下能合理地發揮作用。

Try the test

☐ 1. I do not like their carrot-stick policy.

☐ 2. I do not like their carrot-and-stick policy.

1. ✕ 2. ✓

99　與 sick 搭配的常用語

sick 是 "患病" 的意思。例如：

> His mother is very <u>sick</u>.
> 他母親病得很厲害。

> Mary had been off <u>sick</u> for ten days.
> 瑪麗因病十天沒上班了。

> Peter has just called in <u>sick</u>.
> 彼得剛才打電話來請病假了。

它也是 "想嘔吐" 的意思。例如：

> If you eat any more cake, you'll make yourself <u>sick</u>.
> 你要是再吃蛋糕，就會吐了。

sickness 是名詞。例子：

> He has been off work because of <u>sickness</u>.
> 他因病沒上班。

morning sickness 是 "晨吐"，即 "孕婦在早晨作嘔" 的意思。

> Note："暈車" 是 carsick、"暈船" 是 seasick、"暈飛機" 是 airsick、"旅行暈眩" 是 travel-sick，注意 travel 和 sick 之間有連字符號。但 lovesick 是 "單思病" 的意思。

Try to remember

I was / felt <u>seasick</u>, so I went up the deck for some fresh air.
我有些暈船，所以到甲板上呼吸些新鮮空氣。

He is inclined to be <u>carsick</u>. 他很容易暈車。

Other examples

As I read my mother's letter, I began to feel more and more <u>homesick</u>.
我在讀媽媽的來信時開始覺得越來越想家。

She was moping around like a <u>lovesick</u> teenager.

她像個有單相思病的年青人悶悶不樂地閒蕩。

Try the test

☐ 1. I have carsick.

☐ 2. I am carsick.

1. ✗   2. ✓

100 開支票不可直譯 *open a cheque

cheque 是 "支票" 的意思，與支票搭配的詞組有：

to pay by cheque	用支票付款
to cash a cheque	兌現支票
to open a cheque account	開立支票戶口
to make out a cheque to someone	把支票開給某人
to dishonour a cheque / to bounce a cheque	戶口存款不足兌現不到支票 / 彈票
crossed cheque	劃線支票
blank cheque	已簽署的空白支票
a cheque for $500	一張五百元的支票
to write a cheque	開支票，但不是 to open a cheque，是 to write a cheque

Note：cheque 在美國是 check，等於 bill，是 "賬單" 的意思。例如：

Can I have <u>the check</u>, please?
請把賬單給我好嗎？

Try to remember

I <u>wrote him a cheque</u> for $1,000.

我給他開了一張一千元的支票。

I don't have any cash on me, so could I pay <u>with a / by cheque</u>?

我沒帶現金，能用支票付款嗎？

Other examples

Please <u>make your cheques payable to</u> the Hong Kong Limited.

請把支票開給香港有限公司

He received <u>a cheque</u> from Mr. Chan for $10,000.

他收到陳先生一張一萬元的支票。

Try the test

☐   1. Please open a cheque for $500.

☐   2. Please write a cheque for $500.

1. ✗   2. ✓

101 "冷落某人"英文該怎説？

cold-shoulder 是"冷落、冷待"的意思。例如：

I tried to be pleasant to her but she gave me the cold shoulder.

我努力想討好她，但她反倒故意冷落我。

a cold-hearted killer 是"冷酷無情的殺手"，a cold-blooded murder 是"冷血的謀殺"。

我們對 cold 的本義"冷"不會陌生。例如：

It was bitterly cold outside.

外面非常寒冷。

如果説"涼爽、涼快"，那是 cool。例如：

A cool breeze blew off the sea.

涼爽的海風從海邊吹來。

cool 也是"好的、極妙"的意思，特別用於英語口語，也是年輕一輩常用的詞彙。例如：

She looks really cool in that new dress.

她穿上那件新裙子顯得漂亮極了。

Try to remember

It is freezing cold today.

今天冷極了。

She received a rather cold response.

她得到的反應很冷淡。

Other examples

We were cold-called by a company offering savings on our phone bill.

有家公司給我們打來促銷電話，推銷節省電話費的業務。

We had such a cool time at your party.

我們在你的派對上過得愉快極了。

Try the test

☐　1. When Peter asked Mary for a date, she gave him a cold shoulder.

☐　2. When Peter asked Mary for a date, she gave him the cold shoulder.

1. ✗　　2. ✓

102　豐富多彩的顏色詞

我常説發掘學習英語的興趣，英語就自然容易學得好，舉一個例子，我們可以學會所有顏色詞。colour 是 "顏色、色彩" 的意思。例如：

> What is your favourite colour?
>
> 你最喜歡的顏色是甚麼？

bright / dark / light colour 是 "鮮艷 / 深 / 淺顏色"，a colour TV 是 "彩色電視機"。

它的形容詞是 colourful，是 "顏色鮮艷、五彩繽紛、豐富多彩" 的意思。例如：colourful shop windows 是 "五彩繽紛的商店櫥窗"，a colourful history / past / career 是 "豐富多彩的歷史 / 過去 / 經歷"。

> Note：用顏色形容物品時，像 "黑色的汽車、房屋、裙子" 等，英文不是 a black colour car / house / dress，而是 a black car / house / dress。

含 colour 的常用語不一定與顏色有關，off-colour 就是一個例子，解作 "身體不適"。

Try to remember

> She was wearing a colourful red and yellow dress.
>
> 她穿了一件鮮艷的紅黃相間連身裙。

> There are many colourfully dressed people on Sundays.
>
> 星期日有很多衣着鮮艷的人。

Other examples

In May and June, our garden is full of <u>brightly-coloured</u> flowers.

五六月間，我們的花園到處盛開着色彩鮮艷的花。

You look a bit <u>off-colour</u> today. Have you got a temperature?

你今天看來好像不舒服，有發燒嗎？

Try the test

☐   1. Colourful wallpaper would brighten up the room.

☐   2. Colour wallpaper would brighten up the room.

1. ✓   2. ✗

103　用 cut-throat 形容“割喉競爭”

百貨公司大減價時，我們常遇到或聽到 cut-throat 這個詞語。有人乾脆把它説成“割喉”，即“鬥得你死我活、不擇手段、殘酷”的意思。例如：

He does not like the cut-throat world of politics.
他不喜歡鬥得你死我活的政治圈。

Cut-throat competition in business is common.
商業上無情的競爭很普遍。

The government protects some industries from cut-throat competition.
政府保護一些工業不被捲入殘酷競爭中。

The advertising world can be a very cut-throat business.
廣告行業的競爭會十分殘酷。

> Note：cutting edge 是 “處於領先地位、優勢” 的意思，加 give 在 a cutting edge 之前，是“給某人帶來優勢”。例如：
> We're relying on her to give the team a cutting edge.
> 我們倚賴她給這個團隊帶來優勢。
> 但 cutback 是“削減、減少”的意思。

Try to remember

She did not enjoy working in the cut-throat world of journalism.
她不喜歡在殘酷無情的新聞界工作。

Graduates trying to find jobs are facing cut-throat competition.
求職的畢業生面對着你死我活的競爭。

Other examples

The closure of the factory is the company's biggest single cutback so far.
關閉工廠是公司至今最大的單一削減措施。

Cutbacks in public spending are expected in the next budget.
明年財政預算可能要削減公共開支。

Try the test

☐   1. They were forced to cut through production.

☐   2. They were forced to cut back production.

1. ✗   2. ✓

104   認識與"手"有關的常用語

學習英語時，應先學會常用詞彙。例如：

hand	手
thumb	拇指
index finger / first finger	食指
middle finger	中指
ring finger	無名指
little finger	小指
fingernail	手指甲
fingertip	指尖
knuckle	指節
palm	手掌
wrist	手腕

be / feel all fingers and all thumbs 是"笨手笨腳"的意思。例如：

I am sorry I broke the plate — I am all fingers and all thumbs today.

對不起我打破了碟子，我今天笨手笨腳。

keep one's fingers crossed 是"祈求好運"的意思。例如：

We must just keep our fingers crossed that we will pass the test tomorrow.

我們要為明天測驗祈求及格。

get your fingers burnt 是 "自作自受 / 自食其果" 的意思。

not lift / raise a finger 是 "不願幫忙" 的意思。

Try to remember

We are keeping our fingers crossed that he is going to be O.K.

我們祈求他不會有事。

I am all fingers and thumbs today. That is the third glass I dropp-ed this morning.

我真笨手笨腳。那已是我今早失手摔破的第三隻玻璃杯。

Other examples

She has had her fingers burnt by deals that turned out badly.

她因幾筆糟糕的交易大吃苦頭。

I do all the work around the office — Peter never lifts a finger.

辦公室的工作都是我做的 —— 彼得一點不幫忙。

Try the test

☐ 1. Peter got his fingers severely burnt when that firm went out of business.

☐ 2. Peter got his fingers severely burn when that firm went out of business.

1. ✓   2. ✗

105   green 有多種用法

顏色詞中，green 很常用。例如：

> Wait for the light to turn green.
> 等綠燈亮了才走。

green 也是 "缺乏經驗、環保" 的意思。例如：

> The new trainees are still very green.
> 這些受培訓的新學員經驗尚淺。

> We should try to adopt a greener lifestyle.
> 我們應盡量採取更環保的生活方式。

> Note：作為名詞，它是 "草地" 的意思。例如：
> Children were playing on the village green.
> 孩子們在村中心的草地上玩耍。

與 green 搭配的詞組還有：

green belt	綠化地帶
green card	允許外國人在美國居住和工作的法律證件 / 綠卡
greengrocer	蔬菜水果店
the greenhouse effect	溫室效應
green light	准許、許可

Try to remember

> We're painting the house in blues and greens.
> 我們正把房子漆成藍色和綠色的。

> The council has given the green light to the new shopping development.
> 議會准許了新購物商場發展計劃。

Other examples

> The next ten years, she predicted, would see the greening of Hong Kong.
> 未來十年裏她預測説香港將更注重環境保護。

There is <u>a green belt</u> around Tai Zhong.

台中周圍有個綠化地帶。

Try the test

☐　1. Mother gave us a green light to go on the camping trip.

☐　2. Mother gave us the green light to go on the camping trip.

1. ✗　2. ✓

106　比較 hands-on 和 hand on

隨着近年私立大學學位和副學士學位增加，香港越來越多學生接受高等教育。正因為畢業生太多，他們畢業後很難馬上找到理想工作。有些可能會繼續進修，有些選擇進入職場，由低做起。

hands-on 是 "實踐經驗、實際操作" 的意思。例如：

Many employers consider <u>hands-on</u> experience to be as useful as academic qualifications.

很多僱主認為實踐經驗同學歷一樣有用。

The computer course includes plenty of <u>hands-on</u> training.

這電腦課程包括大量實際操作訓練。

The programme gives students <u>hands-on</u> experience in a hospital.

該課程為學生提供了在醫院實習的機會。

與 hands-on 不同，hand on 是 "傳給、移交" 的意思。

Try to remember

All children are expected to have had <u>hands-on</u> experience of computers by the time they leave school.

所有孩子預期在離開學校時都有實際使用電腦的經驗。

Ninety-nine per cent of primary pupils now have <u>hands-on</u> experience of computers.

99% 的小學生現在都有電腦操作的實際經驗。

Other examples

The government is criticised for not <u>handing on</u> information about missing funds.

政府因沒有說明資金流失而受到批評。

His company car and mobile phone will be <u>handed on</u> to his successor.

他的公司車和手提電話將傳給他的繼任人。

Try the test

☐   1. Please read this notice and hand on.

☐   2. Please read this notice and hand it on.

1. ✗   2. ✓

107　handsome 有時與 "英俊" 無關

handsome 形容男人外貌英俊。例如：

He's the most <u>handsome</u> man I've ever met.

他是我見過最英俊的男人。

但我們要留意，它也可形容女子，是 "健美" 的意思。例如：

A lot of men said Demi Moore was a tall, <u>handsome</u> woman.

很多男人説狄美摩亞是個高大的健美女子。

它也可以形容動物和物件，是 "美觀、悦目" 的意思，像 a handsome horse / house / city 是 "漂亮的馬 / 房子 / 城市"。也有 "數量大、可觀" 的意思，像 a handsome profit / reward 是 "可觀利潤 / 獎賞"。例如：

He was elected by a <u>handsome</u> majority.

他以高票當選。

Try to remember

Did you see that <u>handsome</u> woman in her fifties?

你看到那個五十多歲的健美女子嗎？

It is a piece of <u>handsome</u> furniture.

這是一件造型美觀的傢具。

Other examples

Her father said if her results were good, he would reward her <u>handsomely</u>.

她父親説若她成績好，他將會大大獎賞她。

Ford expects <u>handsome</u> profits from its business.

福特公司期望從它的業務獲取可觀利潤。

Try the test

☐　1.　$10,000 is quite handsome birthday present.

☐　2.　$10,000 is quite a handsome birthday present.

1. ✗　　2. ✓

108　with great force 不可直譯"大力"

很多人以為懂得翻譯，英文就會好，那可不一定。最重要的是，不要以為中英 "對號入座" 就能學好英語。我們常說的 "大力"，用 with great / a lot of strength / force 表達是不太好的，因那不是習慣用法。"大力" 其實是 "用力、猛烈"，即英文的 hard，是形容詞，也是副詞。例如：

a good hard kick	狠狠一踢
a hard push	用力一推
kick sth very hard	猛踢某物
raining harder than ever	雨下得比任何時候大

Try to remember

I was trying very hard to remember her name.

我很努力嘗試記起她的名字。

You need to push harder.

你要再用力推一下。

Other examples

Small firms in particular were hard hit by the recession.

小公司特別受到衰退的嚴重影響。

I think they will be hard to gain support.

我覺得他們很難獲得支持。

Try the test

☐　1. It was a summer night and raining hard.

☐　2. It was a summer night and raining hardly.

1. ✓   2. ✗

109 "請自便" 英文該怎説 ?

在日常飲食場合裏常説 help yourself / somebody to something,那是 "為 (自己 / 某人取用)" 的意思。例如:

If you want another drink, just help yourself.
你想再喝一杯就請自便。

Can I help you to some more salad?
再給你來點沙律好嗎 ?

Can I have a drink? Help yourself.
我能喝杯酒嗎 ? 自己倒吧。

Let me help you to some more soup.
讓我給你再添些湯。

'Might I have some more water?' 'Please, help yourself.'
"我能再喝些水嗎 ?" "請自便。"

> Note: help out / help somebody out 是 "幫助某人擺脱 (困境)" 的意思。例如:
> When I bought the house, my brother helped me out with a loan.
> 我買這所房子時,我哥哥借了我一筆錢應急。

Try to remember

'Do you mind if I use your phone?' 'Help yourself.'
"我能用一下電話嗎 ?" "請用。"

'Do you want some cake?' 'Help yourself.'
"你想吃蛋糕嗎 ?" "自己拿吧。"

Other examples

She always helped out with the housework.
她總是幫忙做家務。

My family has always helped me out.
我家人總會幫我。

Try the test

□   1. Peter got up and help himself with more wine.

□   2. Peter got up and help himself to more wine.

1. ✗   2. ✓

110   學習含 high 的常用詞組

high 可用作形容詞，除了 "高"，如 high winds 是 "大風" 的意思，說某人 high，是指他 / 她喝醉了。例如：

The trees blew over in the <u>high</u> winds.

樹被大風颳倒了。

She was <u>high</u> on New Year eve.

新年前夕她喝醉了 / 很興奮。

還有其他與 high 搭配的常用語，例如：

high noon	正午
high summer	盛夏
high chair	嬰兒椅子
highbrow newspapers	格調高雅的報紙
highbrow readers	品味高雅的讀者
a high-class restaurant	一家高級餐廳
high-flyers	有抱負、有能力的人
highlight	最精彩的部分、高潮
high tea	傍晚茶

此外，high 也可用作名詞，例如：

The high lasted all night.

那種快感持續了一夜。

He was on a real high after winning the competition.

他贏了那場比賽後高興極了。

Try to remember

The fence is too high to climb over.

圍欄太高，爬不過去。

Some of the waves are 15 feet high.

有些浪高達 15 呎。

Other examples

Teachers no longer enjoy the high social status they once had.

教師已不像過去享有崇高社會地位。

They are giving a high priority to social welfare in their campaigns.

在競選活動中，他們都把社會福利列為優先考慮。

Try the test

☐　1. He's flying high, but he'll fall soon.

☐　2. He's high flying, but he'll fall soon.

1. ✓　2. ✗

111 "跳飛機" 英文該怎説？

遊樂場常見的遊戲，有跳飛機、滑梯、鞦韆、平衡板、旋轉木馬、跳飛機、摩天輪和過山車，它們的英語是甚麼呢？

hopscotch	跳飛機
slide	滑梯
swing	鞦韆
roller coaster	過山車
big wheel	摩天輪
see-saw	平衡板 / 蹺蹺板
roundabout / merry-go-round	旋轉木馬

The children were playing hopscotch in the garden.

他們正在花園玩跳飛機。

He was going down the slide.

他在溜滑梯。

The kids were playing on the swings.

孩子們在盪鞦韆。

They went for a ride on the roller coaster / big wheel.

他們正在玩過山車 / 摩天輪。

They want to play on a see-saw / roundabout / merry-go-round.

他們想玩蹺蹺板 / 旋轉木馬。

Note：seesaw 可以是動詞。

Try to remember

Do you want to have a go on the swing?

你想盪鞦韆嗎？

The children seesawed in the park.

孩子在公園裏玩蹺蹺板。

Other examples

He was on an emotional roller coaster for a while when he lost his job.

他失去工作後有段時間情緒總是大起大落。

Try the test

☐　　1.　She was playing with the swing.

☐　　2.　She was playing on the swing.

> 1. ✗　　2. ✓

112　hot 可以與 "熱" 無關

相信大家對 hot 很熟悉，它是 "熱" 的意思。例如：

It is hot today, isn't it?

今天很熱，對嗎？

Be careful — the plates are hot.

當心 —— 盤子燙手。

I touched her forehead. She felt hot and feverish.

我摸了摸她的前額，感到很燙，是在發燒。

但 hot 不一定與 "熱" 有直接關係，像形容女性 "性感"。

She's hot alright.

她很性感。

也可以用 hot 來形容激烈的競爭，例如：

Competition is getting hotter day by day.

競爭日趨白熱化。

與 hot 搭配的常用語還有：

hot potato	燙手山芋，即 "棘手問題"
hot seat	處於困難
hot meal	熱菜飯
hot spicy food	辛辣食物
hot issue	熱門話題
hot favourite	熱門
an hot actress	當紅女演員
in hot water	陷於困境

Try to remember

After all that running, she was / felt hot.

猛跑一陣後，她很熱 / 覺得很熱。

Making that complaint could get you into hot water.

那樣抱怨會使你處境尷尬。

Other examples

The abortion issue is a political hot potato in the United States.

墮胎問題在美國是個棘手的政治問題。

As soon as the situation becomes too hot, he gets out.

情況一旦過於危險，他便會退出。

Try the test

☐   1. Mexican food is usually more hot.

☐   2. Mexican food is usually very hot.

1. ✗   2. ✓

113　學習含 do 和 make 的常用語

我們做家務，英語是在 house 之前加 do，即 do (the) housework。例如：

I don't like doing housework.

我不愛做家務。

I spent the whole morning doing the housework.

我整個上午都在做家務。

"家務" 又可以説是 household chores。例如：

We share household chores.

我們分擔家務。

> Note：口語裏，常用動詞 do 表達做各種家務。例如：
> | do the dishes | 洗碗碟 |
> |---|---|
> | do the kitchen floor | 刷廚房地板 |
> | do / set the table | 擺放餐具 |

Let me do the dishes / do the cleaning.

我來洗碗碟 / 清潔地方。

He would do the kitchen floor / do the ironing / do the vacuuming.

他來刷廚房地板 / 熨衣服 / 吸塵。

It's your turn to do the table / do the shopping.

輪到你擺放餐具了 / 購物。

> Note：擺放餐具，除 do the table 之外，也可説 set the table。
> 我們也可以用 make 表達做某些家務。例如：
> | make the bed | 鋪牀 |
> |---|---|
> | make breakfast | 做早餐 |

Try to remember

In my family, we share the housework between us.

在我們家，我們分擔家務。

I hate doing housework.

我討厭做家務。

Other examples

If you <u>do the washing up</u>, I'll do the drying.

要是你洗碗，那麼我就抹碗。

She <u>made some coffee</u> for us.

她為我們煮了些咖啡。

Try the test

☐   1.   You and I can do some sightseeing, till I go back to Canada.

☐   2.   You and I can have some sightseeing, till I go back to Canada.

1. ✓   2. ✗

114   說 "為甚麼" 不一定用 why

我們問別人 "為甚麼？怎麼會？"，除了 Why?、Why is it?、How can it be that...? 和 for what reason 之外，非正式說法是 How come? 它也可以表示驚訝。例如：

'I think you owe me some money.' '<u>How come</u>?'

"我想你欠我一些錢呢。" "怎麼會呢？"

<u>How come</u> she got the job when he was the best-qualified person?

他是資歷最佳的人選，怎麼得到職位的會是她？

Note：How about...? 與 How come 沒有關係。How about...? 是 "詢問情況如何……" 的意思。例如：

I'm not going. <u>How about</u> you?
我不打算去。你呢？

<u>How about</u> a break?
休息一下好嗎？

<u>How about</u> going for a meal?
去吃飯好不好？

Try to remember

So <u>how come</u> you got an invitation and not me?
為甚麼你得到邀請而我沒有？

'I don't think I'll be able to go swimming tomorrow.' '<u>How come</u>?'
"我想明天我不能去游泳了？" "為甚麼呢？"

Other examples

<u>How about</u> trying to expand our Japanese market?
我們試着擴展一下日本市場怎麼樣？

Are your products and services competitive? <u>How about</u> marketing?
你們的產品和服務有優勢嗎？推廣又如何？

Try the test

☐ 1. How about you are late?

☐ 2. How come you are late?

1. ✗   2. ✓

115 記住與 **make** 經常搭配的名詞

我們常説 "做、作出"，英語是 make。它與某些名詞連用，表示完成與該名詞相關的動作。例如：

make a decision	決定
make a call	打電話
make a mistake	犯錯
make a suggestion	提建議
make reservations	預訂
make a commitment	承諾
make a contribution / donation	捐獻 / 捐款
make money	賺錢
make a living	謀生
make a profit	獲利

Peter will try to make a decision by Monday.
彼得將設法在星期一前作出決定。

Can I use your mobile phone to make a call?
我可以用你的手機打個電話嗎？

I really feel he's making a mistake.
我真的認為他正犯錯。

Can I make a suggestion?
我可以提個建議嗎？

You need to make reservations at least two weeks in advance.
你需要至少提前 2 個星期預訂。

He refused to make a commitment.
他拒絕作出承諾。

She made a contribution / donation to The Red Cross.
她對紅十字會作出捐獻 / 捐款。

His father was the only breadwinner who <u>made money</u> to support the family.

只有他父親一個人掙錢養家。

Can you <u>make a living</u> doing this?

靠做這個你足以謀生嗎？

The company is not likely to <u>make a profit</u> this year.

該公司看來不能在今年獲利。

Try to remember

I must <u>make a call</u> to my office.

我要給辦公室打個電話。

You're not <u>making any effort</u> — try harder.

你沒盡力 —— 加把勁。

Other examples

Don't <u>make any noise</u>.

別出聲。

I'll just <u>make certain</u> that I've turned the oven off.

我要確定一下烤箱是否已關掉。

Try the test

☐   1. Can I make suggestion?

☐   2. Can I make a suggestion?

1. ✗   2. ✓

116　學習含 mind 的常用語

我們常說 decide，它是 "決定、拿主意" 的意思。此外，也可說 make up your mind。例如：

Have you made up your mind what to do yet?

你已拿定主意做甚麼嗎？

You will never persuade her to stay — her mind has made up.

你根本無法勸她留下 —— 她已拿定主意。

They are both beautiful — I cannot make up my mind.

兩個都很漂亮 —— 我難以決定。

> Note：bear in mind 是 "記住" 的意思。例如：
>
> You must bear in mind that their customs are very different to ours.
> 你必須記住他們的風俗習慣跟我們的不太一樣。
> It slipped my mind. / It went (right) out of my mind.
> 我一點也記不起來。/ 我已忘得一乾二淨。

Try to remember

I haven't made up my mind where to go yet.

我還沒有打定主意去哪裏。

My mind is made up — I am leaving!

我已下定決心，我要離開。

Other examples

It's over. Put it out of your mind.

結束了。你忘了它吧。

He's very strong. / He's independent-minded.

他果斷。/ 他有獨立見解。

Try the test

☐　1.　She made her mind not to say a word.

☐　2.　She made up her mind not to say a word.

1. ✗　2. ✓

117　記住 mean 搭配 by, any harm

不明白別人意思時，除了説 What do you mean? 外，還有其他説法，例如：

> What do you <u>mean</u> by 'data collection'?
>
> data collection 是甚麼意思？

其實，在日常會話，mean 很有用。例如：

> What he <u>means</u> is that there is no point in waiting here.
>
> 他的意思是説在這裏等下去也沒意思。

> I see what you <u>mean</u>, but I still think it's worth trying.
>
> 我知道你是甚麼意思，但我仍認為它值得一試。

> I am sorry I hurt you. I didn't <u>mean</u> to.
>
> 對不起弄痛了你，我不是故意的。

Try to remember

> Did she <u>mean</u> it when she said she had burnt the letter?
>
> 她説已把信燒了，是真的嗎？

> I've been <u>meaning</u> to phone you for a week.
>
> 我已想了一個星期要打電話給你。

Other examples

> I am sorry if I offended you — I didn't <u>mean</u> any harm.
>
> 如果我冒犯了你，請多原諒 —— 我並無惡意。

> It isn't <u>meant</u> to be difficult.
>
> 別故意搞得那麼難。

Try the test

☐　1. I realised what he meant.

☐　2. I realised what he means.

1. ✓　　2. ✗

118 "大杯子、搶劫、傻" 都可用 mug

去年有人冒認我向朋友發出電郵，説我在旅行時被搶劫，急需 2,000 美元的援助。我最記得那句 I was <u>mugged</u>. ，因為許多香港人都知道"嘜"就是 mug，即 "大杯、缸子"。例如 a coffee mug / beer <u>mug</u>，但它也是動詞，即 "搶劫、打劫" 的意思。其他例子：

They had been <u>mugged</u> in the street in broad daylight.

光天化日之下，他們在街上遭搶劫。

mugging 是名詞。例如：

<u>Mugging</u> is on the increase.

搶劫犯罪呈上升趨勢。

mugger 是 "搶劫犯、攔路搶劫者"。

> Note：He's no mug. 是 "他不傻。" 的意思。mug 用作動詞時是 "扮鬼臉" 的意思。

Try to remember

Every New Yorker expects to be <u>mugged</u> sometime.

每個紐約人都可能在某時刻遭搶劫。

I made myself a large <u>mug</u> of coffee.

我為自己沖了一大杯咖啡。

Other examples

He is such a <u>mug</u>, he believes everything she tells him.

他真傻，無論她説甚麼他都相信。

Kids <u>were mugging</u> for the camera.

孩子正在鏡頭前扮鬼臉。

Try the test

☐　1. Give the baby a mug with milk.

☐　2. Give the baby a mug of milk.

1. ✗　　2. ✓

119　指別人"故意"不一定用 on purpose

要英文作文寫得好，要懂得用慣用語作為詞彙以外的另一種變化。例如，說"故意、有意"，可以用 intentionally 和 deliberately。但也可以說 on purpose 或 purposely。例如：

> She did it on purpose, knowing it would annoy him.
> 她明知會激怒他，卻故意那麼做。

> 'I'm sorry I stepped on your toes; it was an accident.'　'It wasn't! You did it on purpose.'
> "對不起！我踩到了你的腳趾頭。""我不是故意的。""不！你是存心踩的。"

> The police believe the fire was set on purpose.
> 警方相信有人故意放火。

> She came here on purpose to see him.
> 她特地來這裏看他。

Try to remember

> I didn't do it on purpose. It was an accident.
> 我不是故意這樣做的，是個意外。

> I purposely avoid making train journeys during rush hours.
> 我有意避開在繁忙時間乘火車。

Other examples

> Did you leave her name by accident or was it intentional?
> 你漏掉她的名字是無意的還是有意的？

> I'm sure she's well-intentioned — she wouldn't mean any harm.
> 我確信她是善意的 —— 她不會有任何惡意。

Try the test

☐　1. I am sorry I hit you; it was no intention.

☐　2. I am sorry I hit you; it was not intentional.

1. ✗　2. ✓

120 "有朝一日"英文該怎說？

我們常説"有朝一日、總有一天"，英語是 one day / some day。例如：

> One day, I want to leave him.
>
> 有朝一日，我要離開他。
>
> Some day, we will take a trip to Russia.
>
> 總有一天，我們會到俄國旅行。

one of these days 是 "將來有一天" 的意思。例如：

> You are going to get into serious trouble one of these days.
>
> 將有一天你會惹上大麻煩。

另外，at the end of the day 是 "最終、到頭來" 的意思。例如：

> At the end of the day, it is the government's responsibility to stop this sort of thing from happening again.
>
> 到頭來，制止這類事的發生仍是政府的責任。
>
> At the end of the day, he will still have to make his own decision.
>
> 最終，他還得自己拿主意。

day in and day out 是 "日復一日" 的意思。

Try to remember

> One day the truth will be known about Kennedy's murder.
>
> 有朝一日，暗殺甘迺迪事件會真相大白。
>
> I would love to go to Japan some / one day.
>
> 將來有一天，我要去日本。

Other examples

> One of these days, I will leave and never come back.
>
> 將來有一天，我將離開，而且將不再回來。
>
> I have to do the same boring jobs day in and day out.
>
> 我每天都要做這些單調乏味的工作。

Try the test

☐   1. I'll call on you one of these days.

☐   2. I'll call on you one of the days.

1. ✓   2. ✗

121 "憂鬱、發青、突然"都可用 blue 表達

我們知道 blue 是 "藍色" 的意思。例如：

a blue shirt	藍色襯衫
blue-collar workers	藍領工人
blue eyes	藍色眼睛

但 blue 也是 "青紫、發青" 的意思。例如：

His hands were blue with cold.

他雙手凍得發青。

作為非正式的用法，blue 是 "憂鬱、悲傷" 的意思。例如：

He has been feeling blue all week.

他整個星期都情緒低落。

> Note："色情片"中文叫"黃色電影"，但不可直譯為 *a yellow movie，正確的英文是 a blue movie。

out of the blue 是 "出乎意料、突然" 的意思。例如：

The decision came out of the blue.

這個決定來得很突然。

含 blue 的常用語還有：

blue-chip companies	藍籌公司
blue-eyed boy	寵兒
blueprint	藍圖
bluetooth	藍牙
once in a blue moon	少有，罕見

Try to remember

The plane shot off into the blue.

飛機直衝上天。

A lot of women get the blues after the baby is born.

許多婦女生完孩子之後患上抑鬱症。

Other examples

My brother lives in France, so I only see him once in a blue moon.

我哥哥住在法國，因此我很少見到他。

One day, out of the blue, she announced that she was leaving.

有一天，她突然宣佈要走。

Try the test

☐　1.　I'm felt blue all day.

☐　2.　I've felt blue all day.

1. ✗　2. ✓

122   學習 hand 的多種用法

hand 有很多用法。例如：

on the left-hand side	在左面
on the right-hand side	在右面
left-handed	慣用左手
right-handed	慣用右手
right-hand man	左右手 / 得力助手
empty-handed	空手
heavy-handed	形容政府或管理層 "高壓、專橫"
high-handed	專橫
hand in hand	手牽手
give / lend somebody a hand	幫忙

Try to remember

He's right-handed.

他習慣用右手。

Susan returned home empty-handed from her shopping trip.

蘇珊出去購物，結果空手而回。

Other examples

Could you give / lend me a hand with the sofa, please?

你能幫我搬一下這張沙發嗎？

I saw them walking hand in hand in the garden the other day.

那天我看見他們手牽手走過花園。

Try the test

☐   1. He gave me a hand moving the piano.

☐   2. He gave me a hand in moving the piano.

1. ✗   2. ✓

123　same 常後接 as 或 that

same 有以下的用法：

在 the、this、that、these、those 之後用作形容詞。例如：

> We both went to the same school.
>
> 我們上同一間學校。

在 the 之後用作代名詞或副詞。例如：

> I'd do the same if I had the chance.
>
> 如果有機會，我也會做同樣的事。

> The twins always dress the same.
>
> 這對雙胞胎總是穿得一樣。

> Note：the same 常後接 as 或 that。例如：
>
> I have got the same problem as you have.
> 我的問題和你的一樣。
> It is the same film that they saw last month.
> 這是他們上月看過的同一部電影。

在非正式口語中，有時會省略 same 之前的 the。例如：

> We'll meet again next week, same time, same place.
>
> 我們下星期再見，老時間、老地方。

> It is the same old story.
>
> 一直都是這樣。／又是老一套。

Try to remember

> She was wearing exactly the same dress as I was.
>
> 她穿的裙子和我的一模一樣。

> It rained every day of our holiday — but we had a good time all the same.
>
> 假期裏天天下雨 —— 不過我們仍然玩得很開心。

Other examples

'Have a good holiday.' 'Same to you!'

"假日愉快。""也祝你假日愉快。"

It is the same old story — the rich get richer and the poor get poorer.

還是老一套 —— 富人越富，窮人越窮。

Try the test

☐   1. The chairman is of the same opinion.

☐   2. The chairman is the same opinion.

1. ✓   2. ✗

124   seldom, often 等頻度副詞的使用規則

很多人不清楚頻度副詞 often、usually、sometimes、never、rarely、seldom 的使用規則。

1) 句中只有一個動詞，頻度副詞應放在動詞前面，例如：

I usually walk to school.

我經常走路上學。

2) 句中動詞詞組有兩部分，頻度副詞應放在詞組中間，例如：

I have never been to Japan.

我從沒去過日本。

3) 句中動詞只有一個 be 動詞，頻度副詞是在 be 動詞後面。

She is never punctual.

她從不準時。

4) 句中有 not，頻度副詞是在 not 後面，例如：

She doesn't <u>usually</u> go by bus.

她很少乘搭巴士去。

> Note：為了強調，這些頻度副詞可放在句首。例如：
> <u>Sometimes</u> we take food with us and sometimes we buy food when we are there.
> 有時，我們自己帶食物，有時我們在那裏買。

Try to remember

I don't <u>often</u> drink spirits.

我不常喝烈酒。

We <u>rarely</u> see each other now.

我們現在很少見面。

Other examples

<u>Sometimes</u> it is best not to say anything.

有時候，最好是甚麼話都別説。

<u>Seldom</u> do we receive any apology when mistakes are made.

出錯的時候，我們很少聽到道歉的説話。

Try the test

☐   1. Does usually she go to you for advice?

☐   2. Does she usually go to you for advice?

1. ✗   2. ✓

125 "衣衫襤褸" 英文該怎説？

表達一個人衣衫襤褸，或形容建築物、衣服、物品等破破爛爛，可以用 old、broken 或 poor，但最貼切生動的形容詞是 shabby。例如：

He wore shabby old jeans and a T-shirt.

他穿着一條破舊牛仔褲和一件 T-恤。

I saw a shabby old tramp in the rear lane last night.

昨晚我在後巷看見一個衣衫襤褸的老流浪漢。

> Note：shabby 也是 "不光彩" 的意思。
>
> 　　　另外，與它相似的 shaggy 是 "頭髮蓬亂" 的意思。例如：
> 　　　She has a shaggy mane of hair.
> 　　　她的長髮亂蓬蓬的。
> 　　　He has a shaggy white dog.
> 　　　他有一頭皮毛亂蓬蓬的大白狗。

Try to remember

He wore an shabby old overcoat.

他穿着一件破舊大衣。

The boat people were shabby and hungry.

那些船民衣衫襤褸、飢腸轆轆。

Other examples

I felt the whole affair was a bit shabby.

我感覺整件事有點不光彩。

I feel I behaved shabbily.

我覺得我表現得很不光彩。

Try the test

☐　1. His old suit looks shaggy.

☐　2. His old suit looks shabby.

1. ✗　2. ✓

126   small 不一定解作 "小"

我常鼓勵同學閱讀詞典，一個有效方法是從詞典尋找有用的詞彙短語，抄錄在自己的筆記簿上方便溫習。small 除了解作 "細小" 外，搭配其他詞語會有不同意思：

small talk	聊天
small beer（Brit.）/ potatoes（Am.）small fry	小人物或不重要的人或事物
the small hours	凌晨
small-minded	固執己見
small claims tribunal	小額錢債審裁處
It's a small world.	世界真細小，真湊巧（意外遇見某人或發現對方也認識某人時説）

Try to remember

They may be key players in their own company, buy they are small fry in the industry itself.

他們可能是自己公司裏的核心人物，但在整個行業裏卻無足輕重。

He was up until the small hours of the morning to finish her essay.

為了寫完論文，他一直熬夜到凌晨。

Other examples

So you know my old Chinese teacher! Well, it is certainly a small world, isn't it?

原來你認識我以前的中文老師！嘿！這是太巧了，不是嗎？

She has some very small-minded opinions about foreigners.

她對外國人有一些很狹隘的看法。

Try the test

☐   1. He woke up in small hours.

☐   2. He woke up in the small hours.

1. ✗   2. ✓

127   表達"喝采"不一定用 great

表示感歎語氣，可用形容詞修飾名詞。例如：

Spectacular!	好！
Great!	精彩！
Cool!	酷！
Fantastic / Terrific / Brilliant / Tremendous / Awesome / Wonderful!	了不起！/ 棒極了！

Peter scored a spectacular goal.
彼得射了一個精彩入球。

What a great goal!
這球入得精彩！

'How's the concert?' 'It's cool.'
"音樂會怎樣？" "棒極了！"

You look fantastic in that dress!
你穿着那件連衣裙看起來棒極了！

You look terrific!
你看起來棒極了！

'How was it?' 'Brilliant!'
"怎麼樣？" "棒極了！"

It was a tremendous experience.
這是個了不起的經歷。

Wow! That's totally awesome!
哇！真是棒極了！

It is a wonderful performance.
這是精彩的演出。

Try to remember

There was a spectacular sunset last night.
昨晚的日落非常壯觀。

They've won a holiday? How <u>fantastic</u>!

他們贏得了一個假期？太棒了！

Other examples

You won? That's <u>tremendous</u>!

你贏了？棒極了！

We had a <u>wonderful</u> time in Japan last week.

上星期我們在日本玩得非常開心。

Try the test

☐   1. This is a fantastic dessert.

☐   2. This is fantastic dessert.

1. ✓   2. ✗

128   still 是形容詞也是副詞

寫記敍文和描寫文時，常說 "靜止、動也不動"，英文是 still，是形容詞和副詞。例如：

Keep <u>still</u> while I cut your hair.

我給你剪頭髮時，你不要動。

The kids found it hard to stay <u>still</u>.

孩子們覺得很難待着不動。

Can you sit <u>still</u>?

你就不能安安靜靜地坐一會嗎？

如果我們説一切活動停止、停頓，那是 standstill。例如：

Traffic in the south-bound lane is at a complete standstill.

南行車道的交通完全停頓。

He brought the car to a standstill.

他把車子停了下來。

still 也是名詞。例如：

In the still of the night, nothing moved.

夜深人靜、萬籟俱寂。

Try to remember

The air was so still that not even the leaves on the trees were moving.

一點風都沒有，連樹葉動也不動。

The water appeared still from a distance.

從遠處看，水是靜止的。

Other examples

Fighting and shortages have brought normal life to a virtual standstill in the city.

戰火和物資短缺使這城市的正常生活瀕臨癱瘓。

The peace process is at a standstill.

和平進程停滯下來了。

Try the test

☐   1. The children can't still for a moment.

☐   2. The children can't keep still for a moment.

1. ✗   2. ✓

129　說"考慮到"不一定用 consider

我們常說"考慮",最簡單的英語是 consider。但為了使文筆有變化,其實可用同義的慣用語 take into account 和 take account of。例如:

> I hope my teacher will take into account the fact that I was ill just before the exams when she marks my paper.
> 我希望老師在閱卷時,能考慮到我恰好在考試前生病這個情況。

> A good architect takes into account the building's surroundings.
> 一個好建築師會考慮到建築物周圍的環境。

> Britain's tax system takes no account of student.
> 英國稅制沒把學生考慮在內。

> I think you have to take into account that she is a good deal younger than the rest of us.
> 我認為你要考慮她比我們其他人年輕多了。

Try to remember

> Compensation awards take into account the pain and suffering caused to the victim.
> 賠償數目已考慮到受害人經歷過的痛苦和折磨。

> If you take inflation into account, we actually spend less now.
> 如果你把通脹因素都考慮進去,我們現在花的錢其實少了。

Other examples

> His exam results were not very good, but we must take into account his long illness.
> 他的考試成績不很好,但我們必須考慮到他曾長期生病。

> The teachers promised to take account of the wishes of the parents before making any changes.
> 教師答應在作出變更之前會考慮家長的願望。

Try the test

☐　1.　You need not take much account of that.

☐　2.　You need not take much an account of that.

1. ✓　2. ✗

130　"從容、隨和、隨便"都可用 **easy**

easy 除了是"容易、輕易"的意思之外,它還解作"舒適、安逸"。例如:

> The doctor told him to go easy / take things easy and stop working so hard.
>
> 醫生勸他要放鬆一下,不要工作過勞。
>
> Just take it easy and tell us exactly what happened.
>
> 別緊張,確實地告訴我們發生了甚麼事。

> Note:easygoing 是"脾氣隨和"的意思。例如:
>
> Our teacher is very easygoing, he doesn't mind if we turn up late.
> 我們的老師非常隨和,我們遲到他都不在乎。

I'm easy. 是非正式說法,它是"隨便、一點不在意",即粵語"是但"的意思。例如:

> 'Would you like tea or coffee?' 'I'm easy.'
>
> "你想喝茶還是咖啡?""我隨便。"

take it easy 是"從容點"的意思。

Try to remember

> She is very easy to talk to.
>
> 她平易近人,跟她很容易談得來。

It isn't <u>easy</u> being a parent.

為人父母殊非易事。

Other examples

Peter is a friendly, <u>easygoing</u> type of guy.

彼得是一個友好隨和的人。

Just <u>take it easy</u> and tell us exactly what happened.

別緊張，確實告訴我們發生了甚麼事。

Try the test

☐   1. Our lives are easy so far.

☐   2. Our lives have been easy so far.

1. ✗   2. ✓

131 "慢慢來"不是用 slow

一些簡單詞語不一定是常於口語裏用，像 slowly。例如：

Could you speak more <u>slowly</u>?

請你説慢一點好不好？

He found that life moved <u>slowly</u> in the countryside.

他發現鄉村的生活節奏慢。

<u>Slowly</u> things began to improve.

慢慢地，情況開始好轉了。

不用 slowly，可以用 take your time 表達 "慢慢來" 的意思。

<u>Take your time</u>. / <u>Take your time</u> to do something / doing something.

慢慢來，不用急。

There is no rush / hurry. <u>Take your time</u>.

不用急，慢慢來。

Just <u>take your time</u> and think about what you are saying and you will be fine.

別急，想想你要説的話，這樣就會好。

Try to remember

They swam <u>slowly</u> across the lake.

他們慢慢游過湖面。

The city is <u>slowly</u> getting back to normal after a three-day transport strike.

運輸業罷工三天後，這城市慢慢恢復正常。

Other examples

You can <u>take your time</u>. It will do if you let me know in an hour.

你可以慢慢來，一小時後告訴我就行了。

Since there was no need to hurry, we <u>took our time</u> leaving.

由於不用急，我們慢慢離開。

Try the test

☐   1. He likes to take his time over breakfast.

☐   2. He likes to take time over breakfast.

1. ✓   2. ✗

132   表達 "……之前" 可用 other

我們常說 "某事在不久之前的日子發生",例如:

the other day	幾天前
the other morning	前幾天早上
the other afternoon	前幾天下午
the other evening	前幾天傍晚
the other night	前幾晚
the other week	前幾個星期

I saw Peter the other day.

我幾天前看到了彼得。

Susan broke her arm the other morning.

前幾天早上蘇珊弄斷了手臂。

The accident happened the other afternoon.

意外在前幾天下午發生。

He lost his wallet the other evening.

前幾天傍晚他遺失錢包。

They left Hong Kong the other night.

前幾晚他們離開了香港。

The other night we had a party.

前幾夜我們舉行了一次聚會。

I rang her the other week.

我前幾個星期給她打過電話。

Try to remember

Didn't I see you at the post office the other day?

前幾天在郵局我不是看到了你嗎？

We visited them just the other week.

我們就在幾星期前拜訪過他們。

Other examples

He phoned me the other night to say he could come.

他前幾夜打過電話給我說他能來。

My sister came down the other evening.

我姐姐前幾晚都來了我這裏。

Try the test

- ☐ 1. I just happened to see her other day.
- ☐ 2. I just happened to see her the other day.

1. ✗   2. ✓

133 比較 ripe 和 mature

ripe 是"水果或穀物成熟"的意思,反義詞是 unripe。例如:

These bananas are not ripe; they will give you indigestion.

這些香蕉不熟,吃了會消化不良。

它也是"適宜、時機成熟"的意思。例如:

The land is ripe for commercial development.

這塊土地適宜發展商業。

The time was ripe for a challenge to the government.

時機成熟,可以向政府提出挑戰了。

> Note:牛排"煮熟"是 done,"熟透"是 well-done,"煮得嫩"是 rare。

但説一個人成熟,英語是 mature 如 a mature student 是成年學生,a mature woman 是成年婦女。反義詞是 immature。例如:

Peter is very mature for his age.

彼得年紀不大,卻很成熟。

Try to remember

The time is ripe to invest in new technology.

為新技術投資的成機成熟了。

The company is ripe for takeover.

公司被接管的條件已成熟。

Other examples

The garden has a lot of beautiful mature oak trees.

花園裏有許多漂亮的成年橡樹。

In Britain, mature students are over 25 years old, and in Australia, they are over 22 years old.

在英國,超過25歲為成年學生,在澳洲,22歲以上即為成年學生。

Try the test

☐　1. Fifty is a mature age.

☐　2. Fifty is mature age.

1. ✓　2. ✗

134　timing 可與 perfect / wrong 等字搭配

不少香港人喜歡談話時中英夾雜，其中一個原因是他們認為有時用英語表達較簡單易明，例如 timing：

timing	時間的掌握、安排或選擇
good / bad timing	時間選擇得當 / 不當

Your timing is perfect. I was just about to call you.

你來得正是時候，我剛想給你打電話。

I don't think much of the timing — introducing a new brand of ice-cream in December.

我認為他們時間選得不好 —— 竟然在十二月推出一款新牌子的冰淇淋。

He is an actor with a great time of comic timing.

他是個懂得把握時機引人發笑的演員。

Try to remember

Have we arrived early? No, your timing is perfect — dinner is almost ready.

我們到得太早了嗎？不，你們來得正好，就要開飯了。

To be a good tennis player, you have to have <u>good timing</u>.

要成為一個優秀的網球運動員，你必須掌握好擊球時機。

Other examples

It was unfortunate <u>timing</u> that my father called just as we were about to go out.

真不湊巧，我們正要出去時，我爸爸打來了電話。

My <u>timing</u> was completely wrong.

我在時間選擇上全錯了。

Try the test

☐   1. The time of last night's performance was excellent.

☐   2. The timing of last night's performance was excellent.

1. ✗   2. ✓

135 "麻煩別人"英文該怎說？

trouble 是名詞，解作"麻煩、問題、困難"，它也可以是動詞，解作"使煩惱"。例如：

> We have trouble getting good staff.
> 我們聘請好員工有困難。

> The trouble with her is she doesn't really want to work hard.
> 她的問題在於她不是真的想勤力工作。

> I don't want to put you to a lot of trouble.
> 我不想增添你很多麻煩。

> I don't want to trouble the doctor with such a small problem.
> 我不想為了一個小問題去麻煩醫生。

trouble 的形容詞是 troublesome，解作"令人煩惱"，如 a trouble-some child / problem 是"令人煩惱的孩子 / 問題"。

Note：troublemaker 是"搗蛋鬼、惹事生非者"。

Try to remember

> May I trouble you for some wine please?
> 請給我一些葡萄酒好嗎？

> Could I trouble you to open the window?
> 能麻煩你打開那扇窗嗎？

Other examples

> Her stammer has been troublesome for her.
> 她的口吃令她很苦惱。

> We can't afford in these troublesome times to have a new Chairman who is weak.
> 在這個困難時期，我們受不住一個軟弱的新主席。

Try the test

☐   1.   The youth was a trouble student.

☐   2.   The youth was a troublesome student.

1. ✗   2. ✓

136   說 "難以置信" 不一定用 unbelievable

對某事或某種情況覺得 "不可思議、難以置信" 時，可以說 unthinkable，它與 unbelievable 和 inconceivable 同義。例如：

It is quite <u>unthinkable</u> that she should be expected to pay the whole cost herself.

期望她自己付所有費用簡直不可想像。

It was <u>unthinkable</u> that he could be dead.

他竟然去世了，真是難以置信。

Suddenly the <u>unthinkable</u> happened and she drew out a gun.

突然，難以置信的事發生了，她拔出了手槍。

You can't imagine what it would be like to have your child die — it's quite <u>unthinkable</u>.

你想像不出如果一個人失去了孩子會怎樣 —— 那是不能想像的。

Try to remember

For most people in Japan, the prospect of war is <u>unthinkable</u>.

對日本大多數人來說，戰爭的前景是無法想像的。

Nowadays wines are being produced in areas that would have been <u>unthinkable</u> even twenty years ago.

現今葡萄酒正在二十年前甚至無法想像的地區生產。

Other examples

Ten years ago, interest rates in excess of 20 per cent would have been <u>unthinkable</u>.

在十年前，利率超過 20% 會是不可思議的。

In late 1997, the <u>unthinkable</u> occurred, the company went bankrupt.

1997 年末，不可思議的事發生了，公司竟然破產了。

Try the test

☐   1.   It would be unthinkable to ask her to do that.

☐   2.   It would unthink to ask her to do that.

1. ✓   2. ✗

137 口語裏 what 的多種用法

在英文口語裏，What for？很常用，是"為何目的，為何理由"的意思。
例如：

'I am going to Japan.' '<u>What for</u>?'

"我要去日本。""<u>去做甚麼</u>？"

'<u>What</u> did you <u>do that for</u>?'

"你為何做那事？"

'<u>What's</u> this thing <u>for</u>?'

"這個東西有甚麼用？"

'I need to see a doctor.' 'What for?'

"我要去看醫生。""為甚麼？"

What about...? 是 "如何、怎麼樣……" 的意思。例如：

What about a drink?

喝杯酒如何？

What about you, Peter? Do you like basketball?

你怎麼樣，彼得？你喜歡打籃球嗎？

What if...? 是 "要是……會怎樣？"。例如：

What if the train is late?

火車要是遲了會怎樣？

Try to remember

What about Susan — shall we invite her?

蘇珊呢 —— 我們該不該邀請她？

What about taking a few days off?

休幾天假怎樣？

Other examples

What if she doesn't pass her exams?

要是她考試不合格怎辦？

What if he doesn't come?

要是他不來怎辦？

Try the test

☐   1. She asked what was it for.

☐   2. She asked what it was for.

1. ✗   2. ✓

138　white 不一定解作 "白色"

white 是 "白色" 的意思。例如：

white paint	白油漆
white rice	白色的大米
white with fear / anger	氣 / 嚇得臉色發白
white-collar	白領階層
white-collar union / workers	白領階層的工會 / 白領工作者
white elephant	白象
white knight	白武士（為某公司提供資金，使之免受另一公司收購，救急的人或組織）
white lie	無傷大雅的謊言
white paper	白皮書，即英國政府就某些打算要處理的問題向國會提出正式報告

Try to remember

She is white-haired now.

她現在頭髮都已白了。

He turned white and began to stammer.

他臉色變得蒼白，開始結結巴巴地説話。

Other examples

In some countries, it is traditional for a bride to wear white.

在某些國家的傳統中，新娘要穿白色禮服。

The government is trying to whitewash the incompetence of the high-ranking officials.

政府正試圖掩飾高級官員的無能。

Try the test

☐　1.　You told him a white lie when you said he looked good.

☐　2.　You told white lie when you said he looked good.

1. ✓　　2. ✗

139   用 yellow 形容性格

各種顏色之中，yellow 較易學。

You should wear more yellow — it suits you.

你應多穿些黃色的衣服 —— 那適合你。

含 yellow 的詞組有不同意思，舉例如下：

yellow pages	黃頁分類商業電話號碼簿
yellow line	規定時間內某些路段不可停車的黃線
double yellow line	雙黃線，表示全天某些路段不可停車
yellow card	足球比賽中的黃牌
yellow ribbon	黃絲帶，繫它在樹上，表示期盼親友早日返回
yellow	膽小

yellowish 是 "淡黃、微黃" 的意思，例如：

The leaves vary from yellowish — green to dark green.

葉子從黃綠色到深綠色，各有不同。

Try to remember

The paper had yellowed with age.

這紙因年久而變黃了。

The fish is dark green on top, with yellowish sides.

這條魚的上面是深綠色，兩側是微黃色。

Other examples

Peter's teeth had yellowed over time.

彼得的牙齒已逐漸變黃了。

I knew you were quiet, but I didn't know you were yellow.

我知道你不太說話，但我不知道你膽小。

Try the test

☐   1. The newspaper had yellowed by sunlight.

☐   2. The newspaper had been yellowed by sunlight.

1. ✗   2. ✓

140　表示"擊打"不一定用 hit

我們先學手部動作，表示"用手或器具擊打"，常用的英文是 hit。例如：

She hit him on the head with her umbrella.

她用雨傘打他的頭。

strike 是"大力擊打"。例如：

He struck the table with his fist.

他用拳頭打桌子。

beat 是"反覆地打"。例如：

A young boy was found beaten to death.

有人發現一個少年被打死了。

beat up 是"痛毆、毒打"。例如：

He was beaten up by a thug.

他被一個暴徒毒打。

slap 是"用手掌打"。例如：

She slapped his face hard.

她狠狠給了他一個耳光。

smack 是"用巴掌打人"，尤用於打孩子。

I'll smack your bottom if you don't behave.

如果不規矩點，我便會打你的屁股。

Try to remember

Teachers are not allowed to hit their pupils.

不允許教師打學生。

The clock was striking five as we went into the church.

我們走進教堂時，響起了五點報時的鐘聲。

Other examples

When his ideas were rejected, he <u>slapped</u> his report (down) on the table.

他的想法被否決後，他就把報告摔在桌上。

They saw her <u>beating</u> her dog with a stick.

他們看見她用棍子打她的狗。

Try the test

☐   1. He hit the man in the head.

☐   2. He hit the man on the head.

1. ✗   2. ✓

141 記住與 bend 連用的介詞

bend 這個動詞很實用，首先它可以形容我們的身體或頭部傾斜或偏向。例如：

He <u>bent</u> and kissed the kid.

他低下頭吻了那小孩。

Peter <u>bent over</u> to pick up the newspaper.

彼得彎腰去撿起報紙。

Susan was <u>bent over</u> her desk writing a letter.

蘇珊正伏案寫信。

He <u>bent</u> the wire <u>into</u> the shape of a square.

他把鐵絲折成正方形。

The road <u>bent</u> sharply to the left.

路向左急彎。

The branches <u>bent</u> in the wind.

樹枝被風吹彎了。

> Note：bend 也是名詞。例如：
> There is a sharp <u>bend ahead</u> in the road.
> 路前面有急彎。

含 bend 的慣用語有 bend the truth，是"扭曲事實、歪曲事實"的意思。

Try to remember

He <u>bent down</u> and picked up the coins lying on the road.

我彎腰撿起路上的硬幣。

Now, <u>bend forward / over</u> and touch your feet.

現在向前彎腰，觸摸腳趾。

Other examples

Can't you <u>bend</u> the rules a little?

你就不能稍微變通一下嗎？

The local council was forced to <u>bend</u> to public pressure.

地方議會被迫屈從於公眾壓力。

Try the test

☐　1.　The nurse bent down and kissed the child.

☐　2.　The nurse was bent and kissed the child.

1. ✓　　2. ✗

142   記住含 break 的常用語

我們大力把一些東西弄破、碎裂，英文是 break。例如：

All the windows <u>broke</u> with the force of the blast.

爆炸的巨大力量震碎了所有窗戶。

He fell off a ladder and <u>broke</u> his arm.

他從梯子上掉下來，摔斷了胳膊。

She <u>broke</u> the chocolate into two.

她把那塊巧克力一分為二。

break 也是"弄壞"的意思。例如：

My watch was <u>broken</u>.

我的錶壞了。

I think I have <u>broken</u> the washing machine.

我想我弄壞了洗衣機。

> Note：break the law / rules / conditions 是"違反法律 / 規則 / 條件"的意思。
> break an agreement / a contract / a promise / your word 是"違反協議 / 合同 / 允諾；食言"的意思。
>
> He <u>was breaking</u> the speed limit.
> 他違例超速駕駛。

Try to remember

The plate fell to the floor and <u>broke</u>.

碟子跌到地上摔破了。

We heard the sound of <u>breaking</u> glass.

我們聽到玻璃破碎的聲音。

Other examples

She didn't know she <u>was breaking</u> the law.

她不知道她在犯法。

He <u>broke</u> his promise / word to me.

他違背了對我的承諾。

Try the test

□   1. I am sorry that I am broken my promise.

□   2. I am sorry that I broke my promise.

1. ✗   2. ✓

143   catch 不一定解作"捕捉"

catch 很常用。首先它是"捕捉、抓到"的意思。例如：

>   The murderer was never <u>caught</u>.
>   這個殺人犯一直未抓到。

>   Our cat is hopeless at <u>catching</u> mice.
>   我們的貓絕對捉不到老鼠。

>   How many fish have you <u>caught</u>?
>   你捕到幾條魚？

catch 也是"接住、趕上、染病和碰見"的意思。例如：

>   The dog <u>caught</u> that stick in its mouth.
>   狗銜住了木棍。

>   I must go — I have to <u>catch</u> the bus.
>   我要走了 —— 我要趕公共汽車。

>   He thinks he must have <u>caught</u> this cold from you.
>   他說他的感冒想必是你傳染的。

>   I <u>caught</u> him smoking in the classroom.
>   我撞見他在課室裏抽煙。

The thief was caught in the act.

那竊賊在偷竊時被當場抓住。

Try to remember

I managed to catch the glass before it hit the ground.

我在玻璃杯掉到地上以前把它抓住了。

He caught hold of her arm.

他一把抓住了她的手臂。

Other examples

Something bright had caught the baby's attention.

一樣很亮的東西吸引了那個嬰兒的注意力。

Don't try to talk, sit down and catch your breath.

不要説話，坐下來喘喘氣。

Try the test

☐   1. She caught me to smoke a cigarette.

☐   2. She caught me smoking a cigarette.

1. ✗   2. ✓

144 記住含 chop 的常用語

我們常用刀切碎、剁碎食物，英文是 chop。例如：

Chop the carrots up into small pieces.

把胡蘿蔔切成小塊。

chop 也是"砍、劈"的意思。例如：

He was chopping logs for firewood.

他在把原木劈成木柴。

作為非正式用語，chop 是"取消、削減"的意思。例如：

The government has chopped funding for the arts.

政府已不再提供藝術活動經費。

含 chop 的常用語還有：

pork / lamb chop	豬 / 羊排
chopping board	砧板
chopper	大砍刀 / 小斧頭 / 菜刀 直升機（非正式用語）
chop-chop	快、趕快

Try to remember

Most of the diseased trees were chopped down last year.

大部分病樹在去年被砍倒了。

Because of lack of funding, many long-term research projects are being chopped.

因為缺乏資金，許多長期研究項目被砍掉了。

Other examples

The company has chopped another 350 people from the staff.

公司又從職員中裁減 350 人。

Come on, chop-chop, we haven't much time before the train goes.

趕快，快點快點，我們沒有多少時間，火車快要開了。

Chop-chop! We haven't got all day.

快！快！我們時間無多。

☐   1. The fireman chopped a hole in the wall.

☐   2. The fireman chopped down a hole in the wall.

1. ✓   2. ✗

145   記住與 cut 連用的介詞

cut 十分常用，是 "切、割、割破、劃破" 的意思。例如：

She cut her finger on a piece of glass.

一塊玻璃劃破了她的手指頭。

He cut himself / his face shaving.

他刮鬍子時劃破了臉。

You need a powerful saw to cut through metal.

切割金屬要用功率大的鋸。

cut 也是 "用刀切下、割下" 的意思。例如：

She cut four thick slices from the loaf.

她從一條麵包切下四塊厚片。

I cut a piece of birthday cake for them all.

我為他們每人切了一塊生日蛋糕。

The bus was cut into two by the train.

那輛公共汽車被火車撞成兩截。

Don't <u>cut</u> the string, untie the knots.

別剪斷繩子，解開那個結。

Try to remember

Could you <u>cut</u> me a slice of bread?

能幫我切片麵包嗎？

I have <u>cut</u> myself / my hand with that knife.

我被那把小刀割傷了自己 / 手。

Other examples

They have <u>cut (down)</u> the cost of cleaning the hospital by lowering standards.

他們靠降低標準減少清潔醫院的費用。

The firm has <u>cut back / down (on)</u> wastage / production / labour.

公司削減了損耗 / 生產 / 勞工。

Try the test

☐   1. Cut the apples into half.

☐   2. Cut the apples into halves.

1. ✗   2. ✓

146 "時間拖得太長"英文該怎說

drag 是 "吃力地在地上拖、拉、拽、扯" 的意思。例如：

I dragged the sofa over to the window.

我把沙發拖到了窗戶那邊。

The bag is too heavy to lift — you'll have to drag it.

這袋子太重了，提不起來。你要拖着它走。

drag 也是 "時間過得很慢" 的意思。例如：

The meeting really dragged.

這會議開得真拖拉。

drag on 是 "拖得 / 持續太久" 的意思。例如：

The dispute has dragged on for months.

這場爭論持續了幾個月。

Note：be a drag on... 是 "拖累、成為⋯⋯的累贅"。例如：

He didn't want a wife who would be a drag on his career.

他不想要一個拖累他事業的太太。

Try to remember

Pull the chair up instead of dragging it behind you.

抬起椅子，別把它拖在你身後。

I had to drag the child screaming out of the shop.

我不得不把大叫着的小孩拖出商店。

Other examples

Don't drag me into your argument! It's nothing to do with me.

別拉我參加你們的爭論，這事與我無關。

I don't want to drag out this meeting. So, could we run through the main points quickly?

我不想延長這個會議。這樣，我們能不能迅速將要點過一次？

Try the test

☐ 1. We were dragged them apart to stop the fight.

☐ 2. We dragged them apart to stop the fight.

1. ✗   2. ✓

147 "攪掂"英文該怎說

電影和電視劇裏常用 fix 表達 "整好、攪掂"。fix 是 "修理、修復、解決" 的意思。例如:

The engineer <u>fixed</u> our central heating.

工程師修理了我們的中央空調系統。

The car can't start — can you <u>fix</u> it?

這部車發動不起來了 —— 你能修理一下嗎?

He <u>has fixed</u> the problem.

他已解決了這個問題。

> Note:fix 也是 "安排、決定、確定" 的意思。例如:
> The date of the next meeting <u>has been fixed</u> on 7 April.
> 下次會議日期已確定在四月七日。
> They <u>fixed</u> the rent at $10,000 per month.
> 他們把租金定為每月 10,000 元。

Try to remember

Will you <u>fix</u> the shelf to the wall?

你可否把架子釘到牆上?

Shall we fix (up) a time for the next meeting?

我們可否將下次開會的時間定下來？

Other examples

Give me a couple of minutes while I fix my hair.

等我兩三分鐘讓我整一整頭髮。

The ballot was fixed.

投票結果是預先安排好的。

Try the test

☐   1. The tables were firmly fixed to the floor.

☐   2. The tables firmly fixed to the floor.

1. ✓   2. ✗

148　記住與 fold 連用的介詞

我們常用手摺疊、對摺紙張和布等，英文是 fold。例如：

Fold the paper along the dotted line.

沿虛線把紙摺起來。

It will fit if you fold it in half.

對摺的話就放得下。

She folded the map up and put it in her pocket.

她把地圖摺疊起來放進了口袋。

The blankets had been folded down.

毛毯已摺疊起來。

fold your arms 是 "交叉雙臂"。例如：

Peter stood silently with his arms folded.

彼得交叉着雙臂，一言不發地站着。

fold 也是 "倒閉" 的意思。例如：

1,000 small businesses were folding every year.

每年有 1,000 家小公司倒閉。

Try to remember

I folded the letter (in half) and put it in an envelope.

我對摺了信，放進了信封。

Will you help me to fold up the sheets?

可否幫我疊起這些牀單？

Other examples

He folded his arms and tried to look stern.

他叉起雙臂盡力顯出一副嚴肅的神情。

Make sure the umbrella is dry before folding it.

切記要等雨傘乾了再收攏起來。

Try the test

- ☐ 1. The paper must fold in half.
- ☐ 2. The paper must be folded in half.

1. ✗　2. ✓

149　記住含 hand 的常用語

很多短語動詞和慣用語含 hand，如 hand in 是"呈交、提交"的意思。
例如：

Please <u>hand in</u> your assignment tomorrow.
請在明天交功課。

The manager has threatened to <u>hand in</u> his resignation unless his
demands are accepted.
經理威脅説他的要求若不獲接納就會辭職。

hand in hand 是"手拉手、緊密合作"的意思。例如：

The boy and girl were walking along <u>hand in hand</u>.
那男孩和那女孩手拉手地走着。

Doctors and nurses work <u>hand in hand</u> to save lives.
醫生和護士緊密合作拯救生命。

> Note：go hand in hand 是"一起發生的意思"。例如：
> A bad economic situation and rising crime usually <u>go hand in hand</u>.
> 經濟不景和犯罪率上升通常一起發生。

live hand to mouth 是"剛夠糊口"的意思。

Try to remember

Prosperity goes hand in hand with investment.

繁榮與投資密切相連。

We have been living hand to mouth ever since I lost my job.

自從我失了業，我們的收入僅夠糊口。

Other examples

I have got enough money in hand to buy a new car.

我手上有足夠的錢去買一輛新車。

Would you hand the cake out while I pour the coffee?

可否我一邊倒咖啡，你一邊把蛋糕分給在場的每個人？

Try the test

☐ 1. They sat down, close together, hands in hands.

☐ 2. They sat down, close together, hand in hand.

1. ✗   2. ✓

150　表示"抓緊"不只可用 **hold on**

乘坐公共汽車抓緊扶手或椅背，英文是 hold on。例如：

She held onto the back of the chair to stop herself from falling.

她扶住椅子後背，以免摔倒。

He held on tightly to the rail.

他緊緊抓住了把手。

hold on 的同義詞 clutch，解作"用手抓緊、突然抓住"。例如：

She felt herself slipped and clutched at a branch.

她感到自己滑了一下，便抓住一根樹枝。

grasp 是"抓緊、抓牢"。例如：

He grasped my hand and shook it warmly.

他熱情地抓着我的手握了起來。

grip 是"用手緊握"，grip the rope 是"緊握繩子"。

> Note：聽電話時說 hold on，是"等一下、別掛斷"的意思。

Try to remember

Please hold on / hold tight / hold on tight the rail while the bus is in motion.

公共汽車行駛時，請抓牢 / 緊緊抓住 / 緊抓住把手。

Terrified by the noise, the small child clutched (onto) his father's hand.

那小孩被喧鬧聲嚇壞，緊緊抓着他父親的手。

Other examples

He grasped me by the arm and led me to the window.

他抓住我的手臂，拉我到窗口。

The baby gripped my finger with his tiny hand.

這個嬰兒用他的小手抓緊我的手指。

Try the test

☐   1. Hold, everything will be all right.

☐   2. Hold on, everything will be all right.

1. ✗   2. ✓

151   將 "手" 的相關詞串連學習

用手接觸有不同方法，feel 是 "摸、觸摸" 的意思。例如：

I felt the bag to see what was in it.

我摸摸提包，看了看裏面有甚麼東西。

rub 是 "揉、搓、擦" 的意思。例如：

She rubbed her eyes wearily.

她疲倦地揉了揉眼睛。

stroke 是 "輕撫、撫摸" 的意思。例如：

The dog loves being stroked.

這狗喜歡別人輕撫。

pat 是 "輕拍" 的意思。例如：

She patted my arm and told me not to worry.

她輕輕拍了我的手臂，叫我別擔心。

tap 是 "輕擊、輕敲" 的意思。例如：

Someone was tapping lightly at the door.

有人在輕輕敲門。

Try to remember

Peter rubbed the blackboard clean for the teacher.

彼得為老師擦淨了黑板。

He <u>stroke</u> the kid's face with the tips of his finger.

他用手指尖撫摸那小孩的臉。

Other examples

She <u>patted my head</u> / <u>patted me on the head</u>.

她拍拍我的頭。

I could hear him <u>tapping</u> his fingers on the desk.

我聽到他用手指輕叩桌子的聲音。

Try the test

☐   1. She gave the dog a pat as she walked out.

☐   2. She gave the dog patted as she walked out.

1. ✓   2. ✗

152 表示 "摘、挖、剔、挑選" 用 pick

pick 是 "採、摘、挑、撿、揀、挖、剔、挑選" 的意思，比 pluck 更常用。例如：

She picked some flowers from the garden.

她從花園裏採摘了一些鮮花。

He picked her a rose.

他採了一朵玫瑰花給她。

He was picking bits of glass out of the carpet.

他撿拾地毯上的碎玻璃。

Don't pick your nose!

不要用手挖鼻孔。

She was picking her teeth.

她正在剔牙。

The students have to pick four courses from a list of 10.

學生必須從十科中選修四科。

> Note：pick 也是 "偷、扒竊" 的意思。例如：
>
> It is easy to have your pocket picked in a big crowd.
> 身處一大群人之中，你口袋裏的東西很易被人扒掉。
>
> pick holes 是 "找毛病、缺點" 的意思，另有 pick on，是 "故意挑剔" 的意思。例如：
>
> He was picked on by other boys because of his size.
> 他因為個子關係被其他男孩故意挑剔。

Try to remember

One of my classmates were picked for the school team.

我的一個同班同學獲選參加校隊。

He sent to pick up the phone, but it had stopped ringing.

他去接電話，但它不再響了。

Other examples

Last week, she <u>had her pocket picked</u> by the man sitting next to her in a café.

上星期，她在一家咖啡室裏被坐在旁邊的一個男人偷了錢包。

He didn't take the proposal seriously and just spent half an hour <u>picking holes</u> in it.

他不認真看待那份建議書，只花了半個小時來挑它的缺點。

Try the test

☐　1. We picked the best room among those available.

☐　2. We picked up the best room among those available.

1. ✓　2. ✗

153　表示"學會、接送、搭訕"用 pick up

pick 有多個很有用的短語動詞。pick up 是"接送"的意思。例如：

The bus <u>picks up</u> passengers outside the airport.

公共汽車在機場外接送乘客。

Peter will <u>pick me up</u> at the gate.

彼得將會在大閘接我上車。

pick 也是"得到、學會"的意思。例如：

She <u>picked up</u> French when she was living in Paris.

她旅居巴黎時，順便學會了法語。

在非正式場合，可用 pick 表示"搭訕、勾搭"的意思。例如：

He goes to the club to <u>pick up</u> girls.

他到俱樂部去泡妞。

Note：pick 也是提高增加的意思。

Try to remember

The nurse had picked up the information from a conversation she overheard.

護士從她偶然聽到的對話中得知這個消息。

People see this period as a good time to pick up bargains.

人們以為這段時期是買便宜貨的好時機。

Other examples

We don't expect the number of applicants to pick up until at least the spring.

至少在春天前，我們預期申請的人數不會增加。

The car picked up speed slowly.

那汽車慢慢加速。

Try the test

☐   1. Pick me at the hotel.

☐   2. Pick me up at the hotel.

1. ✗   2. ✓

154　穿耳 / 鼻 / 舌環英文該怎說

拿尖的物體 "刺入、刺破、刺穿或穿透" 另一個物體，英文是 pierce，是動詞。例如：

The arrow pierced his shoulder.

箭頭射穿他的肩膀。

He pierced another hole in his belt with his knife.

他用刀在皮腰帶上又刺了一個洞。

現在流行在耳朵 / 鼻子 / 口唇 / 肚臍 / 舌頭上穿孔，以便戴上珠寶首飾，那是 to have your ears / nose / lip / navel / tongue pierced。例如：

Many women have got ears pierced.

許多女士都給耳朵穿了孔。

The knife pierced through his coat.

刀刺穿了他的外衣。

但 pierce 不一定指真實的刺穿，還可以比喻某人心裏傷心難過。

She was pierced to the heart with guilt.

她萬般愧疚，心如刀割。

Note：pier 雖與 pierce 拼寫相似，在意義上沒有關係，pier 是 "碼頭" 的意思。

Try to remember

I couldn't wear these earrings because my ears aren't pierced.

我不能戴這些耳環，因為我的耳朵沒穿過孔。

He pierced the skin of the potato with a fork.

他用叉子戳破馬鈴薯的皮。

Other examples

We shivered in the piercing wind.

我們在刺骨的寒風中顫抖。

The flashlights pierced the darkness like fireflies.

閃光燈的光像螢火蟲一樣穿透黑暗。

Try the test

☐   1. The needle pierced into his skin.

☐   2. The needle pierced his skin.

1. ✗   2. ✓

155   表示"摘、拔、掐"用 pluck

我們常説"摘、拔、掐、拔掉、用手指猛揪、拉扯",英文是 pluck。例如:

He plucked out a grey hair.

他拔掉了一根灰白頭髮。

He plucked a rose for his girl friend.

他為女友摘了一朵玫瑰花。

She plucked an apple from the tree.

她從樹上摘了一個蘋果。

Do you pluck your eyebrows?

你修眉嗎?

The little girl plucked at his sleeve to try to get his attention.

這小女孩不停地拉他的衣袖,嘗試吸引他的注意力。

pluck 也是"拯救"的意思。

至於 pluck up (one's / the) courage 是"鼓起勇氣、振作精神"的意思。

例如:

She couldn't pluck up enough courage to ask him to go out with her.

她未能鼓起足夠勇氣邀請他一起外出。

Try to remember

She plucked the letter from my hand, and ran off with it.

她從我手裏搶過信就跑開了。

Ships in the area plucked 100 people from the sea.

在該海域的船從海裏救起了 100 個人。

Other examples

He finally plucked up courage to ask her to marry him.

他終於鼓起勇氣向她求婚。

I'd love to make a bungee jump, but I can't pluck up enough courage.

我很想玩笨豬跳，但膽量不夠。

Try the test

☐   1. He plucked up the courage to speak to her.

☐   2. He plucked the courage to speak to her.

1. ✓   2. ✗

156　將名詞和搭配動詞串連學習

學英文名詞時，應同時記住經常搭配的動詞，有助實際應用。例如，我們常用手指來指向某人或某東西，英文是 point。

point 是 "指、指向" 的意思。例如：

He pointed to the house on the corner.

他指着拐角處的房子。

It is rude to point at people.

用手指指人沒禮貌。

> Note：point to 是 "非故意、無敵意的指向"。
>
> It is rude to point!
> 用手指指着別人很不禮貌！
> He pointed to the place where he found the boy.
> 他指出他找到那男孩的地方。

point at 是 "瞄準、故意指向" 的意思。例如：

He pointed the gun at her head.

他舉起槍瞄準她的頭。

'What is your name?' she asked, pointing at the child with her pen.

她用筆指着小孩問："你叫甚麼名字？"

Try to remember

'Look at that!', he said, pointing at the hole in the door.

"看那個！" 他指着門上的洞說道。

There was an arrow pointing to the door.

有個箭頭指向房門。

Other examples

She said that the man had pointed a knife at her.

她說那男人用刀指着她。

All the cars were pointing in the same direction.

所有汽車都朝一個方向行駛。

Try the test

☐   1. Point the gun to the target.

☐   2. Point the gun at the target.

1. ✗   2. ✓

157 "用手指戳" 英文該怎説

我們用手指或物件戳戳點點，英文是 poke。例如：

Don't <u>poke</u> someone in the eye with your umbrella!

傘尖不要戳到別人的眼睛！

poke at something 是"撥弄、戳"的意思。例如：

She <u>poked at the noodles</u> with a fork.

她用叉子撥弄着麵條。

poke 也是"伸出來、探出來"的意思。例如：

Susan <u>poked her head round</u> the door to say hello.

蘇珊從門後探出頭來打招呼。

> Note：poke 也可用作名詞。例如：
> She <u>gave me a poke</u> in the back.
> 她戳了戳我的背部。

poke fun at 是"拿……開心、奚落、嘲弄"的意思。例如：

Her novels <u>poke fun at</u> the upper class.

她的小説嘲弄上流社會。

Try to remember

Two kids <u>were poking</u> a stick into the drain.

兩個孩子把一根棍子插到排水渠裏去。

Peter <u>poked at</u> the vegetables with his chopsticks.

彼得用筷子撥弄着蔬菜。

Other examples

The first green shoots <u>are poking up</u> the soil.

第一批綠芽破土而出。

Mom <u>poked her head</u> into my room and said lunch was ready.

媽媽把頭探進我的房間，説午飯已經做好。

Try the test

☐　1.　The three boys poked fun with the little girl.

☐　2.　The three boys poked fun at the little girl.

1. ✗　2. ✓

158 表示"分開、撬開"用 prise

我們用手強行分開、掀開或用工具撬開物件，英式英語是 prise，美式英語是 pry 或 prize。例如：

He used a knife to <u>prise</u> open the lid.

他用刀撬開蓋子。

The fireman used a crowbar to <u>prise</u> open the car door.

消防員用鐵筆撬開車門。

We <u>prised</u> the top off the box with a lever.

我們用槓桿撬開箱蓋。

A monkey was trying to <u>prise open the lid</u> of the garage can.

猴子嘗試掀開垃圾桶的蓋。

The car trunk <u>had been prised open</u> and all his equipment was gone.

汽車行李箱被撬開了，他所有裝備都不見了。

Try to remember

He <u>prised the lid</u> off with a spoon.

他用勺子撬掉了蓋子。

The window <u>had been prised open</u> with an iron bar.

窗戶被人用撬棍撬開了。

而 prise something out of somebody 是 "費力地從某人那裏獲得消息或金錢"。例如：

She's so secretive — you'll have a hard time <u>prising any information out of her</u>.

她守口如瓶 —— 你很難從她那裏打聽情況。

但是 pry into 和 "分開物件" 無關，是 "窺探" 的意思。例如：

He was hired to <u>pry into</u> her lives.

他受僱去窺探她的生活。

As a private detective, I was sometimes paid to <u>pry into</u> other people's lives.

作為一個私家偵探，有時我收取報酬去窺探別人的生活。

此外，pry 加 -ing 可與 eyes 搭配為 prying eyes，意思是"窺視的目光"。例如：

The movie star could not avoid the <u>prying eyes</u> of the media.

那電影明星無法避開傳媒窺視的目光。

Try the test

☐   1. Stop prying my affairs.

☐   2. Stop prying into my affairs.

1. ✗   2. ✓

159 表示"拖、拉、牽引"用 pull

pull 很常用，是"拉"的意思，指向某方向"拖、拉、牽引"的意思。例如：

Pull the chair nearer the window.

把椅子再往窗口那邊拉近些。

Don't pull so hard or the handle will come off.

別太用力拉，不然把手會脫掉。

Stop pulling her hair.

別揪她的頭髮。

Pull the door shut.

拉上門。

Pull the curtains — it is dark outside.

外邊天黑了，拉上簾。

Try to remember

Could you help me move this table over there? You pull and I will push.

你能幫我把這桌子移到那邊去嗎？你拉我推。

The dentist pulled both teeth out.

牙醫拔了兩顆牙。

但部分含 pull 的慣用語與"拉"的動作沒有太大關係，pull yourself together 是"使自己鎮定或冷靜"的意思。例如：

Just pull yourself together. There's no point crying about it.

要控制自己的情緒，沒必要為了那件事哭。

Try the test

☐ 1. She pulled her car at the gate.

☐ 2. She pulled up her car at the gate.

1. ✗   2. ✓

160 記住與 pull 連用的介詞

許多介詞與 pull 連用，表示不同的意義。例如：pull down 是 "拆卸建築物" 的意思，pull up 是 "車輛或司機停車" 的意思，例如：

They pulled down the warehouse to build a new supermarket.

他們拆了倉庫來興建一家新超級市場。

He pulled up at the traffic lights.

他在交通燈處停車。

Pull the plug out.

拔掉插頭。

She pulled off the boots.

她脫下了靴子。

pull over 是 "車輛駛到路邊"，例如：

Just pull over here, and I will get out.

就在這裏停，讓我下車。

但 pullover 是套頭毛衣，套衫，即 "過頭笠"。

Try to remember

A car pulled up outside my house.

一輛汽車在我家門外停了下來。

He pulled out the drawer.

他拉開了抽屜。

Other examples

It was a crisis year for the company, but we have pulled through.

對公司來說，這是艱難的一年，但我們還是渡過了難關。

Is it really your car or are you pulling my leg?

這真是你的汽車還是你在騙我？

Try the test

□   1. I think you're pulling my leg.

□   2. I think you're pulling my legs.

1. ✓   2. ✗

161   表示"拳打"不用 fist

很多人知道"拳頭"是 fist，但它不是動詞，"拳打"的動詞是 punch。
例如：

He punched me.

他用拳頭打我。

He punched the man in the chest / on the nose.

他一拳打在那男人的胸上 / 鼻子上。

punch 也是名詞，與 give 搭配用，即 give sb a punch。例如：

She'd like to give that man a punch on the nose / in the face.

她想對着那男人的鼻子 / 臉上猛擊一拳。

> Note：punch 也是"打孔"的意思。例如：
>
> The ticket-collector punched my ticket / punched a hole in my ticket.
> 收票員給我的車票打了孔 / 在我的車票上打了個孔。

其他 punch 的例子包括：

punch	打孔機
punch	賓治酒
punch bag	"沙袋"，即拳手練習用的沙包
roll with the punches	泰然接受、隨遇而安

Try to remember

She punched him in the stomach.

她朝他的肚子上猛擊一拳。

Two men punched him, knocking him to the ground.

兩名男子用重拳把他打倒在地上。

Other examples

Peter punched a button on the television.

彼得按下電視機上的一個按鈕。

Being an actor isn't easy, but I've learnt to roll with the punches.

當演員不容易,但我已學會隨遇而安。

Try the test

☐   1. He punched the man on the nose.

☐   2. He punched the man in the nose.

1. ✗   2. ✓

162 表示"推、擠、按"用 push

push 是 "推、推動" 的意思。例如：

> We pushed and pushed but the sofa wouldn't move.
> 我們推了又推，但沙發動也不動。

> The rise in interest rates will push prices up.
> 利率上升將推高物價。

push 也是 "擠、按" 的意思。例如：

> Try and push the way through the crowd.
> 試着從人群中擠過去。

> He pushed the button for the top floor.
> 他按了到頂樓的按鈕。

在非正式場合裏，可用 push 表示 "施壓"。例如：

> His parents are very tolerant, but sometimes he pushed them too far.
> 他父母十分寬容，但他有時也令他們忍無可忍。

> Note：push-up 是 "掌上壓" 的意思，是美式英語，英式英語則是 press-up。
> 多用複數。

Try to remember

> Push as hard as you can.
> 用盡你的全力推。

> She was pushing a trolley around the supermarket.
> 她正推着手推車在超級市場裏四處走。

Other examples

> Susan pushed her handkerchief into her pocket.
> 蘇珊塞了手帕入口袋裏。

> He pushed open the door with his foot.
> 他用腳踹開了門。

Try the test

☐   1. We are pushing them for an answer.

☐   2. We are pushing them to an answer.

1. ✓   2. ×

163   表示"搓、磨、擦"用 rub

用手或物體使勁地搓、磨、擦、揉或撫摸另一個物體的表面，英文是
rub。例如：

He yawned and <u>rubbed</u> his eyes sleepily.

他打着呵欠，睡意矇矓地揉着眼睛。

She <u>rubbed</u> (at) the stains on her dress and made it worse.

她擦裙子上的污漬，結果越擦越髒。

They <u>rubbed</u> some polish into the surface of the wood.

他們在木頭表面刷了一些亮光漆。

Susan <u>rubbed</u> the blackboard clean for the teacher.

蘇珊替老師擦乾淨黑板。

> Note：rubber 是"橡皮"，即 eraser，香港人叫"擦紙膠"，rubber band 是"橡
> 皮圈、橡皮筋"。

rubber-stamp 是"橡皮圖章、例行公事地通過"的意思，可用作名詞及
動詞。

Try to remember

Peter gently <u>rubbed</u> her back until the pain went away.

彼得輕輕按摩她的背，直至疼痛消失。

The cat <u>rubbed</u> its cheek against my leg.

貓臉在我腿上蹭來蹭去。

Other examples

He <u>rubbed</u> some tanning oil on her back.

他幫她在背上抹些防曬油。

I <u>rubbed</u> myself down with a dry towel.

我用乾毛巾擦乾全身。

Try the test

☐   1. He has hurt his leg and he was rubbing.

☐   2. He has hurt his leg and was rubbing it.

1. ✗   2. ✓

164　表示 "抓、刮" 用 scratch

寵物很喜歡抓東西或人，英文是 scratch。例如：

> Be careful the cat doesn't scratch you!
> 當心別讓貓抓傷你！

> The dog is scratching at the door to be let in.
> 這隻狗不斷地抓門想進屋。

scratch 也是 "刮" 的意思。例如：

> I scratched my hand on a rose thorn.
> 我的手被玫瑰刺刮破了。

> The record is badly scratched.
> 唱片已嚴重刮損。

> He scratched his name on the tree with a knife.
> 他用刀把自己的名字刮在樹上。

> Note：scratch the surface 是 "僅接觸到……的表面"，一般用於否定句。例如：
> This report is very superficial; it doesn't even scratch the surface of the problem.
> 這些報告非常膚淺，甚至沒接觸到該問題的表面。

Try to remember

> Scratch my back for me please.
> 請幫我抓抓背。

> The tree's branches had scratched her hands and they were bleeding.
> 樹枝刮傷了她的手，傷口在流血。

Other examples

> The decision has left many party members scratching their heads.
> 這個決定令許多黨員大傷腦筋。

Fortunately he walked away from the accident <u>without a scratch</u>.

幸運的是他在意外中安然無恙。

Try the test

☐   1. He escaped with a scratch.

☐   2. He escaped without a scratch.

1. ✗   2. ✓

165   表示 "搖動、顫抖、震驚" 用 shake

用手把人或東西左右或上下搖動，英文是 shake。例如：

Shake the bottle before use.

使用前搖一搖瓶子。

He <u>shook her</u> by the shoulders.

他抓着她的肩膀搖晃。

She <u>shook her hair</u> loose.

她頭一搖頭髮就散開。

He <u>shook his head</u> in disbelief.

他搖搖頭，不相信。

Do people in Japan <u>shake hands</u> when they meet?

在日本，人們見面時握手嗎？

shake 也是 "身體顫抖、震驚" 的意思。例如：

He was <u>shaking with fear</u>.

他嚇得發抖。

She <u>was badly shaken</u> by the news of his death.

聽到他的死訊，她大為震驚。

shaky 是 "岌岌可危" 的意思。例如：

Their marriage looks pretty <u>shaky</u> to me.

在我看來，他們的婚姻關係岌岌可危。

Try to remember

Houses <u>shook</u> as a bomb exploded in the neighbourhood.

炸彈爆炸時附近的房屋震得直搖晃。

His voice <u>shook</u> as he asked her to marry him.

他向她求婚時聲音顫抖。

Other examples

The girl's tragic death <u>shook</u> the entire community.

那個女孩的慘死使整個社區為之震驚。

Be careful — the table is a bit <u>shaky</u>.

小心，那張桌子有些搖晃。

Try the test

☐   1. The earth was shaky.

☐   2. The earth was shaking.

1. ✗   2. ✓

166　表示"粉碎、打破、破壞"用 shatter

一些東西突然破碎、碎裂，英文是 shatter。例如：

> She dropped the vase and it <u>shattered into pieces</u> on the floor.
> 她失手把花瓶掉到地板上摔破了。

> Did you hear the sound of <u>shattering glass</u>?
> 你當時聽到玻璃破碎的聲音嗎？

> The explosion <u>shattered</u> all the windows in the building.
> 大廈所有玻璃都在爆炸中震碎了。

A stone shattered the window 是 "一塊石頭打碎了窗戶"，也可以比喻為 "感情、希望或信念等粉碎、破滅" 的意思。例如：

> Susan's self-confidence <u>was</u> completely <u>shattered</u>.
> 蘇珊的自信心遭徹底粉碎。

> Hopes of reaching an agreement <u>were shattered</u> today.
> 達成協議的希望今天已破滅了。

> Note：shattering news 是 "令人震驚的消息"。

Try to remember

> The blast <u>shattered</u> windows over a wide area.
> 爆炸震碎了一大片地區的玻璃窗。

> The civil war <u>has shattered</u> the country's economy.
> 內戰嚴重破壞該國的經濟。

Other examples

> The windscreen <u>shattered</u>, injuring passengers.
> 擋風玻璃突然碎裂割傷了乘客。

> Noisy motorbikes <u>shattered</u> the peace.
> 吵鬧的電單車聲打破了寧靜。

Try the test

☐　1.　A stone was shattered the window.

☐　2.　A stone shattered the window.

1. ✗　2. ✓

167　表示"用手掌打、拍、摑"用 slap

slap 是"用手掌打、拍、摑"的意思。例如：

She slapped his face hard.

她狠狠打了他一個耳光。

He slapped her hard across the face.

他狠狠打了她一個耳光。

'Congratulations!' he said, slapping me on the back.

"恭賀你！"他拍着我的背説。

slap 也是名詞，可與 give 搭配使用。例如：

The woman gave him a slap across the face.

那女子打了他一個耳光。

slap 的其他常用語：

a slap in the face	一記耳光、侮辱、打擊
a slap on the wrist	警告、輕微的懲罰
slap-happy	嘻嘻哈哈、甚麼都不放在心上
a slap-happy approach to life	嘻嘻哈哈的生活態度

Try to remember

She gave her son a slap for behaving badly.

她因兒子不聽話打了他一巴掌。

The waves slapped against the stone pier.

波浪拍打着石墩。

Other examples

The court has slapped a ban on the video.

法庭斷然查禁了這段影片。

It was a real slap in the face when the bank turned us down.

銀行拒絕貸款給我們真是個打擊。

Try the test

☐   1. He gave her a slap on the cheek and she began to cry.

☐   2. He gave a slap on the cheek and she began to cry.

1. ✓   2. ✗

168　slap 的近義詞是 smack

有讀者問 "用巴掌打" 的英語是甚麼？

我們知道 "用巴掌打、拍、摑" 是 "掌摑、打一巴掌" 的意思。例如：

I never smack my children.

我從不打我的孩子。

If you don't behave, I'll smack your bottoms.

如果你們不守規矩，我就打你們的屁股。

He smacked a fist into the palm of his hand.

他用拳頭啪地猛擊一下手掌。

smack 也是名詞。例如：

You'll get a smack on your backside if you're not careful.

如果你不小心，就打你的屁股。

Sometimes he just doesn't listen and I end up shouting at him or giving him a smack.

有時他就是不聽，我最後只好向他大叫或打他一巴掌。

smack 也是 "打一拳" 的意思。

Note：smack somebody up 是非正式用語，是 "用手狠打、猛摑" 的意思。

Try to remember

I don't believe it is right to smack children when they are being naughty.

我認為孩子調皮時打他們是不對的。

I gave him a smack on the jaw.

我一拳打在他下巴上。

Other examples

Another car smacked into us from behind.

另一輛車從後面狠狠地撞上了我們。

The whole affair smacked of a government cover-up.

整件事有政府企圖掩飾的跡象。

Try the test

☐　1. If you say that again, I'll smack on your face.

☐　2. If you say that again, I'll smack your face.

1. ✗　2. ✓

169　表示"打碎"不一定用 smash

smash 與 shatter 相似，也是"打碎"的意思。例如：

Several windows had been smashed.

幾扇窗戶被打碎了。

She smashed the radio to pieces.

她把收音機摔得稀巴爛。

smash 也是"猛烈撞擊、碰撞、撞開、粉碎"的意思。例如：

The car smashed into a tree.

汽車猛地撞到了樹上。

Peter smashed his fist on the table.

彼得狠狠地把拳頭砸在桌子上。

We had to smash the door open.

我們只能用力撞開門。

Police say they have smashed a major drugs ring.

警方說他們粉碎了一個大販毒集團。

smash 也是名詞，在英國是撞車的意思，如 a car smash。

Note：smashed 與 "打碎" 無關，是俚語，即 "大醉" 的意思。

Try to remember

Rioters ran through the city centre smashing windows.

暴徒穿過市中心砸碎櫥窗。

She dropped her glass and watched it smash to pieces.

她失手掉了杯子，看着它摔得粉碎。

Other examples

He threatened to smash my face in if I didn't give him the money.

他威脅說如果我不給錢他會揍扁我的臉。

The cars collided with a loud smash.

兩車相撞發出一聲巨響。

Try the test

☐　1. Firemen smashed the door.

☐　2. Firemen smashed the door down.

1. ✗　2. ✓

170 "東西斷裂"英文該怎說

突然把一些東西斷開、斷裂、折斷，並且發出聲音，英文是 snap。例如：

She snapped a twig off a tree.

她從樹上折斷一條小枝。

He snapped the stick in half.

他從中間折斷棍子。

The wind snapped the tree in two.

風把樹斷開，一分為二。

Suddenly, the rope snapped.

突然，繩子斷裂了。

The branch he was standing on snapped off.

他當時踩的樹枝一定是突然折斷了。

snap 也是 "拍照、失去控制" 的意思。例如：

A passing tourist snapped the incident.

一個過路的遊客拍下了這事件。

Her patience finally snapped.

她終於忍不住了。

snap your fingers 是 "彈指頭" 的意思。

Try to remember

You'll snap that ruler if you bend it too far.

如果你把那尺子彎得太厲害，它會折斷。

Did you take many snaps while you were away?

你外遊時拍了很多照片嗎？

Other examples

When he asked me to postpone my trip to help him move house, I just snapped.

他叫我推遲旅行幫他搬家時，我一下子就火了。

She was snapping fingers in time with the music.

她和着音樂節拍彈指頭。

Try the test

☐　1.　The handle of the cup snapped off.

☐　2.　The handle of the cup snapped.

1. ✓　2. ✗

171　記住與手指動作有關的詞彙

用手指做的一般動作包括：press，意思是 "按、壓"。press a button /
switch 是 "按下按鈕、按開關"。

squash 是 "壓扁"。例如：

Squash your cans flat before recycling.

壓扁了飲料罐再送去回收。

squeeze 是 "擠、捏、擰" 的意思，to squeeze a tube of toothpaste 是
"擠牙膏"。又例如：

He took off his wet clothes and squeezed the water out.

他脱下濕衣服，擰乾了水。

"用拇指和手指捏、擰" 是 pinch。例如：

She pinched his cheek.

她捏他的臉頰。

"用手指胳肢別人" 是 tickle。例如：

They used to tickle me.

他們過去總是胳肢我。

Note：The sheet tickles. 是 "牀單使人發癢。"，即廣東話 "拮肉" 的意思。

Try to remember

The crowd pressed against the locked doors trying to get into the building.

人群推着上鎖的門，想進入樓裏去。

She accidentally sat on his hat and squashed it.

她不小心坐了在他帽子上，壓扁了它。

Other examples

These shoes are too tight, they pinch (my feet).

這鞋子太緊了，擠住我的腳。

I have got a tickle in the middle of my back.

我背的中間有點癢。

Try the test

☐　1.　Can we squash in?

☐　2.　Can we squeeze in?

1. ✗   2. ✓

172　表示"激起、惹麻煩"英文該怎説

我們常用手把液體或物質攪拌、攪動，那是 stir。例如：

He stirred his coffee with a plastic spoon.

他用塑料調羹攪拌咖啡。

stir 也是"激起強烈感情"的意思。例如：

He was stirred by her sad story.

她那悲慘的故事打動了他。

stir up 是"惹起麻煩、挑起爭吵"的意思。例如：

Peter was always stirring up troubles in class.

彼得總是在班裏惹麻煩。

其他含 stir 的詞組包括：

stir-fry	炒（菜）、爆炒
stirrer	（攪拌液體的）攪棒
stirring	激動人心、令人振奮
a stirring speech / music	令人振奮的演講 / 激動人心的音樂

Try to remember

Use a wooden spoon to stir the sauce.

用木調羹攪拌調料。

A light breeze stirred the leaves lying on the path.

一陣微風撥動了路上的落葉。

Other examples

After five years of recession, the property market is beginning to stir again.

五年衰退後，房地產市場開始再度活躍。

He gave a stirring speech about the importance of solidarity.

他就團結的重要性發表了一篇激動人心的演説。

Try the test

☐   1. I stir up my tea with my spoon.

☐   2. I stir my tea with my spoon.

1. ✗   2. ✓

173   摸動物不説 touch

我們常觸摸很多物體以至動物和其他人，touch 最常用。例如：

Don't touch that plate — it's hot.

別碰那個盤子，燙手。

Can you touch your toes?

你能彎腰碰着你腳趾嗎？

I touched him lightly on the arm.

我輕輕碰了碰他的手臂。

Her dress was so long it was touching the floor.

她裙子太長，拖到地板了。

但我們觸摸動物、物體表面或頭髮等，應該説 stroke。它是＂輕撫＂的意思。例如：

He is a beautiful dog. Can I stroke him?

這狗真漂亮，我可以摸一摸牠嗎？

She stroked his hair affectionately.

她深情地撫摸着他的頭髮。

He stroked his beard reflectively.

他撫弄着他的鬍子在沉思。

Try to remember

The driver just touched the brake and the car swerved.

司機只是碰了碰煞車,車子就突然歪向了一邊。

No thanks. I never touch chocolate.

不,謝謝。我從不吃巧克力。

Other examples

Stroke the dog if you like, it won't bite.

你想摸這狗就摸吧,牠不咬人。

Fireworks started at the stroke of eleven.

十一點正開始放煙花。

Try the test

☐   1. Cats like be stroked.

☐   2. Cats like being stroked.

1. ✗   2. ✓

174 記住 tear 與 off、up、apart 連用

我們 "撕裂、撕碎、扯破、戳破" 某物，英文是 tear。例如：

He tore his jeans on the fence.

他的牛仔褲被籬笆刮破了。

She tore a hole on her dress.

她裙子刮了個窟窿。

She tore the letter in two.

她把信撕成兩半。

Careful — the fabric tears very easily.

小心，這種織物一撕就破。

tear 也是 "扯破、拔掉" 的意思。例如：

The storm nearly tore the roof off.

暴風幾乎把屋頂掀掉。

He tore another sheet from the pad.

他從本子上又撕下一張紙。

> Note：tear up 是 "撕碎、撕毀" 的意思。例如：
> She tore up all the letters he had sent her.
> 她把他寄給她的信都撕了。

Try to remember

I tore my skirt on the chair as I stood up.

我站起來時撕破了裙子。

The employer just tore up the agreement with the union without consultation.

僱主未經協商就撕毀了與工會的協議書。

Other examples

She tore the room apart looking for her ring.

為了找她的戒指，她翻箱倒篋。

He tore (off) a strip of material to make a bandage.

他撕下一塊布料用作繃帶。

Try the test

☐　1. He tore the letter open.

☐　2. He tore up the letter open.

1. ✓　2. ✗

175　表示"紮、拴、捆、打結"用 tie

我們常用線、繩索 "繫、紮、拴、捆、打結、繫上或綁一些物件"。英文是 tie，例如：

Tie this label to your suitcase.

把這個標籤繫在手提箱上。

They tied him to a tree and beat him up.

他們把他綁在樹上狠狠地打。

I kept all her letters tied together with a rubber band.

我把她所有的信用橡皮圈紮在一起。

She tied her hair back when she's jogging.

她慢跑時把頭髮紮在腦後。

He had only a towel tied around his waist.

他只在腰間圍了一條浴巾，

Can you tie your shoelaces by yourself?

你會自己繫鞋帶嗎？

tie 的反義詞是 untie。例如：

She <u>untied the rope</u> and pushed the boat into the water.

她解開繩纜，把小船推入水中。

Try to remember

He <u>tied the ribbon</u> tightly in a knot.

他把絲帶打成了一個緊緊的結。

She <u>has been tied down</u> by having to work every Saturday.

她每星期六都被工作束縛。

Other examples

I'm not free till Wednesday. I'<u>m tied up</u> on Monday and Tuesday.

星期三之前我沒空，我星期一和星期二都脫不開身。

So when are you two going to <u>tie the knot</u>?

那麼你們倆甚麼時候結婚？

Try the test

☐   1. I tied up the sticks together.

☐   2. I tied the sticks together.

1. ✗   2. ✓

176 "拖、拉、扯"英文該怎説

很多人説"拖拖拉拉、拉拉扯扯",其實"拖、拉、扯"三個動作是有區別的。

drag 是"用力拖、拉",通常指在身後地上拖、拽,自己可能背向前面往前拖。例如:

> The sack is too heavy to lift — you'll have to drag it.
>
> 這袋子重得提不起來,你要拖着它走。

pull 是"拉",通常指向某方向拉、牽引。例如:

> Pull the sofa near the TV.
>
> 把沙發再往電視機拉近些。

説用力拉,英文是 tug,即"扯"。例如:

> She tugged at his sleeve to get his attention.
>
> 她拽了拽他的衣袖吸引他的注意。

> The baby was tugging her hair.
>
> 嬰兒直扯她的頭髮。

tug boat 是"拖船"。

> Note:tug 也是名詞。而 tug-of-war 是"拔河比賽"。

Try to remember

> Some legal issues drag on for many years.
>
> 有些法律問題一拖就是很多年。

> She pulls the string of the switch.
>
> 她拉動開關的拉線。

Other examples

> 'You'd better move on,' said the body guard, tugging his elbow.
>
> 保鏢費力拉着他的胳膊説:"你最好走開。"

> Feeling a tug at her sleeve, she turned to see Peter beside her.
>
> 感覺到有人拉她的衣袖,她轉身看到彼得在她身邊。

Try the test

☐   1. The child tugged at the mother's coat.

☐   2. The child pulled at the mother's coat.

1. ✓   2. ✗

177   將“手部動作”的詞彙串連學習

為了增加學習興趣，大家應把相關詞彙集中一起來學習，就像學會用手
接觸的方法後，也應學習手的“小動作”，例如：

wave	揮手
wave somebody goodbye	向某人揮手告別
put up / raise one's hand	舉手
shake hands	握手
clap hands	拍手
clasp hands	十指緊扣

The people on the tram waved and we waved back.
電車上的人揮手致意，我們也向他們揮手。

Put up / raise your hand if you know the answer.
知道答案就舉手。

They shook hands on the deal.
他們達成協議，互相握手祝賀。

The audience clapped their hands in delight.
觀眾高興地拍起手來。

They clasped hands.
他們十指緊扣。

Try to remember

He <u>waved</u> from the window.

他從窗口揮着手。

The teacher <u>waved her hand</u> to tell the children to be quiet.

那位教師抬起手，要學生安靜。

Other examples

She picked up the phone with <u>a shaking hand</u>, expecting bad news.

她用顫抖的手拿起了電話，等待着壞消息的來臨。

He had to do a second encore because the audience <u>was clapping</u> so much.

觀眾鼓掌如此熱烈，他不得不再度獻唱。

Try the test

☐　1. Wave to your father.

☐　2. Wave at your father.

1. ✓　2. ✗

178   記住 wipe 後接 off、out、up

用手、布或其他東西擦、拭、抹、揩或蹭物體的表面，以清除污點或液體，英文是 wipe。例如：

She wipes her hands on a clean towel.

她用一塊乾淨毛巾擦了擦雙手。

Please wipe your feet on the mat.

請在墊子上蹭一蹭腳。

The girl was wiping her eyes with a tissue.

那女孩用紙巾拭擦眼淚。

He wiped the sweat from his forehead.

他擦去額頭上的汗。

She wiped off her make-up.

她擦掉了粧。

> Note：wipe out 是 "一筆勾銷" 的意思。例如：
> You can never wipe out the past.
> 你永遠不能把過去一筆勾銷。

wipe 也可用作名詞，與 baby 搭配使用，baby wipes 解作嬰兒用的 "濕紙巾"。

Try to remember

Have you got a cloth that I can wipe the floor with?

你有沒有我可以用來擦地板的布？

When you have wiped up (the dishes), don't forget to put them away.

你揩乾（盤子）後，不要忘記放好它們。

Other examples

He wiped his mouth with the back of his hand.

他用手背抹了抹嘴。

I need a handkerchief to <u>wipe off</u> the sand.

我需要一塊手帕揩掉沙子。

Try the test

☐　1. We want to wipe off world hunger by 2020.

☐　2. We want to wipe out world hunger by 2020.

1. ✗　2. ✓

179　記住 listen, apply, afraid 的搭配介詞

學好介詞是有方法的，首先是查閱詞典，把介詞常用的解釋和例子抄在筆記本上複習，其次是把與固定介詞連用的動詞或形容詞一起記下來，像 listen to 是 "聽到聲音或別人説話" 的意思。例如：

Are you <u>listening to</u> me?

你在聽我説話嗎？

apply for 是 "申請" 的意思。例如：

He <u>has applied for</u> a job / passport / grant.

他已申請了工作 / 護照 / 撥款。

afraid of 是 "對某人 / 事物害怕" 的意思。例如：

Peter <u>is afraid of</u> dogs.

彼得怕狗。

即是説 listen, apply, afraid 時，須連同後跟的介詞一起記住，如 listen to, apply for, afraid of。

Note：apply to 是 "適用" 的意思。

Try to remember

She just lies on her bed all day <u>listening to</u> loud music.

她就是整天躺在牀上，聽着嘈雜的音樂。

Please <u>apply in</u> writing to the address below.

請向以下地址寄出書面申請。

Other examples

That bit of the form is for UK citizens — it doesn't <u>apply to</u> you.

表格上的那一項是針對英國公民的 —— 它並不適用於你的情況。

I have always been afraid of flying / height / mice.

我一直懼怕飛行 / 畏高 / 怕老鼠。

Try the test

☐   1. We listened the band playing in the park.

☐   2. We listened to the band playing in the park.

1. ✗   2. ✓

180　at 表示 "某事在某處發生"

at 是介詞，常用意思是 "一個人或一件事物在某處、事件發生的時間或時刻"。例如：

He stood at the corner of the street.

他站在街角。

We changed at Central.

我們在中環轉車。

They arrived late at the airport.

他們晚了到機場。

She will be at home all morning.

她一上午都在家。

He met her at the hospital.

他在醫院遇見了她。

They left at 3 o'clock.

他們在三點鐘離開。

We will go to Japan at weekend.

我們將會於週末前往日本。

I woke at dawn.

我在黎明醒來。

She didn't know it at the time of leaving.

她離開時並不知道。

At night you can see the noon.

夜晚可以看見月亮。

Try to remember

We will meet at the entrance / the ticket office / the cinema.

我們在入口處 / 售票處 / 電影院碰頭。

She is the one in red standing <u>at the bar</u> / sitting <u>at the table in the corner</u>.

她就是站在酒吧那裏 / 坐在角落裏桌子旁的那個紅衣女子。

Other examples

The cat came and lay down <u>at my feet</u>.

這隻貓走過來，躺在我腳邊。

What are you doing <u>at Christmas</u> this year?

今年聖誕節你們怎麼過？

Try the test

☐   1. The car is waiting at the gate.

☐   2. The car is waiting on the gate.

1. ✓   2. ✗

181   at 常用作"向着……方向"

在日常生活中，at 常用作"向着、朝……方向"的意思。

aim at the target 是"瞄準靶子"的意思。

He <u>shot at</u> the bird, but missed it.

他對着鳥開槍，但沒打中。

She <u>shouted at</u> the boy.

她對着那個男孩大叫。

<u>Guess at</u> the answer?

猜一猜答案？

I <u>was surprised / amused / pleased at</u> his behaviour.
我對他的行為感到驚訝 / 有趣 / 高興。

She <u>laughed at</u> him / at his joke.
她對着他大笑 / 聽了他說的笑話大笑起來。

He <u>was impatient at</u> the delay.
他對拖延不耐煩了。

She was <u>good at</u> French.
她法語很好。

He was <u>bad at</u> games.
他不擅長玩競技遊戲。

She's <u>a genius at</u> biology.
她在生物學方面是個天才。

Try to remember

They <u>stared / smiled / waved / pointed at</u> us as we walked by.
當我們走過時，他們凝視我們 / 向我們微笑 / 揮手 / 指指點點。

'Look at me! Look at me!', shouted the little girl.
"看着我！看着我！" 小女孩大聲叫道。

Other examples

She is very <u>good at</u> getting on with people.
她很善於與人相處。

I am <u>terrible at</u> all sports / at games.
我甚麼體育項目也不行。

Try the test

☐　1.　She is quite clever at drawing.

☐　2.　She is quite clever in drawing.

1. ✓　　2. ✗

182　表示"所處狀態或正在做的事"用 at

請注意 at 還表示所處狀態或正在做的事。例如：

I never smoke at work / at school.

我在工作時 / 在學校裏從不抽煙。

The two countries are at war.

兩個國家處於交戰狀態。

它也表示價格、比率、水準、年齡、速度等，即 "以……"、"在……" 的意思。例如：

The apples are sold at (a price of) one dollar each.

蘋果每個以一元（的價格）出售。

The temperature stood at 44°C.

溫度在 44 度。

Should people stop working at (the age of) 60?

人們應在六十歲停止工作嗎？

He was driving at 120 kilometres an hour.

他當時正以每小時 120 公里的速度駕駛。

She saw it at a distance.

她在遠處看到它。

Try to remember

He loves watching the animals at play.

他喜歡看動物嬉耍。

I'm not going to buy those shoes at $1,000.

我不想去買那種 1,000 元一雙的鞋。

Other examples

Inflation is running at 4%.

通貨膨脹率目前為 4%。

He denies driving at dangerous speed.

他否認危險駕駛。

Try the test

- ☐　1. Chinese New Year is almost at hand.
- ☐　2. Chinese New Year is almost in hand.

1. ✓　　2. ✗

183　記住含 at 的常用語

at 除了是 "一個人或一件事物在某處、事件發生的時間或時刻" 的意思外，還有特定意思。例如：

at the top / bottom / end of... 是 "在⋯⋯的頂部 / 底部 / 尾部"。例如：

At the top of the stairs, he paused.
到樓梯的最上面，他停了下來。

I'm sorry, Peter's at lunch right now.
對不起，彼得正在吃午飯。

My boyfriend often works at night.
我男友經常在夜間工作。

They go to Midnight Mass at Christmas.
聖誕節他們要參加子夜彌撒。

She gazed up at the sky.
她抬頭凝望天空。

You don't have to shout at me.
你不必朝我叫嚷。

The boys used to throw stones at me.
那些男孩以前常朝我扔石子。

Try to remember

I'm afraid we can only pay you $50 an hour <u>at (the) most</u>.

我恐怕最多只能付給你每小時 50 元。

<u>At worst</u>, we only lose three days because of the strike.

最壞打算是罷工我們只不過損失三天。

Other examples

My car was damaged in an accident last night, but <u>at least</u> no one was hurt.

我的車昨晚在一宗意外中撞壞，但人至少沒受傷。

Even playing <u>at her best</u>, she couldn't beat her opponent.

儘管她盡過最大努力，她還是未能擊敗對手。

Try the test

☐   1. I'm happy to meet you the last.

☐   2. I'm happy to meet you at last.

1. ✗   2. ✓

184 at 和 peep、wink、glare 搭配

我們知道 at 是 "向、朝" 的意思，例如，各種與觀看有關的動詞如 look, glance, peer, peep, stare, wink 和 glare 之後常配上 at。例如：

What is she looking at?

她在看甚麼？

She glanced at the watch.

她匆匆看了錶。

He peered closely at the photograph.

他聚精會神端詳着照片。

He was peeping at her through his fingers.

他從指縫偷看她。

It's rude to stare at other people.

盯着看別人是不禮貌的。

He winked at her, and she knew he was pretending to be angry.

他向她眨眼示意，她於是明白他假裝生氣。

They didn't fight, but stood there glaring at each other.

他們沒有打架，只是站在那裏怒目而視。

Try to remember

The crowds became violent and threw petrol bombs at the police.

人群變得兇暴，並向警察投擲汽油彈。

She pointed at the empty bottles.

她指向那個空瓶子。

Other examples

He left the light in the room on at her request.

他按照她的要求，把房間的燈亮着。

She was at her happiest while playing basketball.

她打籃球時最高興。

Try the test

☐   1. They wondered at his skill.

☐   2. They wondered with his skill.

1. ✓   2. ✗

185   表示 "在某段較長的時間內" 用 in

對於 in 這個介詞，很多英語學習者覺得很難學，但因為 in 用途很大，所以不能不學。為了學好 in，可以根據它不同的意思分幾次學習。

首先，它多用於時間，是 "在某段時間內" 的意思，通常較長。例如：

He was born in 1997.

他生於 1997 年。

She is getting forgetful in her old age.

她現在上了年紀，變得健忘了。

The house was built in the 17th century.

那座房子在 17 世紀建成。

The birds comes in spring / summer / autumn / winter.

那些鳥在春 / 夏 / 秋 / 冬天來到。

I usually see them in the morning / afternoon / evening.

我通常在上 / 下午或傍晚看到他們。

Try to remember

We are going to Japan in April.

我們將在四月去日本。

Some trees lose their leaves in (the) autumn.

有些樹木在秋天落葉。

Other examples

What was it like to be a student in the late 80s?

80 年代末當個學生不知是怎樣的？

She hasn't heard from them in six months.

她六個月沒聽到他們的消息。

Try the test

☐　1. It is two o'clock. I will come in an hour.

☐　2. It is two o'clock. I will come after an hour.

1. ✓　2. ✗

186   表示"某人或物在……之內"用 in

除了表達時間之外，in 可表示"人或東西在容器、地點或地區裏、在……內"。例如：

There are some cups and plates in the cupboard.

碗櫥裏有些杯碟。

There is a hole in the ground.

地上有個洞。

My father was in the kitchen.

我父親在廚房裏。

She took us for a drive in her new car.

她用她的新車載我們去兜風。

I found him sitting in the bed.

我發現他坐在牀上。

Peter spent ten years in prison.

彼得在監獄服刑了十年。

Mr. Chan is in Japan this month.

陳先生這個月在日本。

My sisters live in Canada.

我姐姐目前住加拿大。

Try to remember

There is a bucket in the cupboard under the sink.

在水槽下面的櫥櫃裏有個水桶。

I wish you'd put the butter back in the fridge when you have finished with it.

我希望你用完牛油後把它放回冰箱裏。

Other examples

Sorry I'm late — I got stuck in a traffic jam for half an hour.

對不起我遲到了 —— 我被交通擠塞堵了半個小時。

They live in a cottage in the middle of a wood.

他們住在樹林中央的小屋內。

Try the test

☐   1. I noticed a hole in his coat.

☐   2. I noticed a hole on his coat.

1. ✓   2. ✗

187   表示"進入"用 in

in 也是副詞，它是"在裏面、在內"的意思。例如：

The woman was locked in.

那女子被鎖在裏面了。

She can't drink coffee with milk in.

她不能喝加了牛奶的咖啡。

Please open the box and put the money in.

請打開箱，放錢進去。

in 也是"進入"的意思。例如：

Application must be in by May 31.

申請必須於五月三十一日之前寄到。

He opened the door and went in.

他打開門進去了。

The boys were playing by the river and one of them fell in.

那些男孩子在河邊玩耍時，其中一個突然跌下水裏。

in 又是 "在家裏、在工作地點" 的意思。例如：

Nobody was in when we called.

我們打電話時家裏沒人。

Sorry, Mr. Chan is not in. Please call again later.

對不起，陳先生不在辦公室，請稍後再打電話來。

Try to remember

Could you bring the clothes in for me?

你可否幫我拿衣服進來？

When does your essay have to be in?

你的文章甚麼時候要交？

Other examples

We stood on the harbour for a while watching the ship come in.

我們在碼頭上站了一會，看着船進港。

Would you mind filling in a questionnaire about what you watch on television?

可否請填寫一份關於你看甚麼電視節目的問卷？

Try the test

☐ 1. He paid me in dollars.

☐ 2. He paid me with dollars.

1. ✓   2. ✗

188　表示"一天"用 on

on 是很常用的介詞。首先，它"表示一天或日期"。例如：

She came on Sunday.

她星期日來了。

We usually meet on Tuesdays.

我們通常每個星期二見面一次。

The accident happened on May the first / the first of May.

意外在五月一日發生。

What did you do on your last birthday?

你上次生日做了甚麼？

I saw her in the library on one occasion.

我曾經有一次在圖書館見到她。

請注意以下的正確用法：

Are you free on the afternoon / evening of July the first?

你七月一日下午 / 傍晚有空嗎？

She will leave on Friday morning.

她會在星期五早上離開。

美式英語可以略去 on。例如：

See you Sunday.

星期日見。

Try to remember

Many shops don't open on Sundays.

許多商店星期天不開門。

I am free on Saturdays.

我星期六有空。

Other examples

My birthday is on the 30th of April.

我生日是四月三十日。

Would you mind telling me what you were doing <u>on the afternoon</u> of Friday the 13th of June?

可否告訴我，六月十三日星期五下午你在做甚麼？

Try the test

☐   1. A party was held in New Year's Eve.

☐   2. A party was held on New Year's Eve.

1. ✗   2. ✓

189   表示"在、向、對"某位置用 on

on 除了顯示日期和日子之外，還常描述"在、向、對……方向、地方和位置"。例如：

There is a picture <u>on the wall</u>.

牆上有幅畫。

Look at the diagram <u>on page 6</u>.

看看第六頁那幅圖。

Put it down <u>on the floor</u>.

放它在地上。

The hotel is <u>on the left / right</u>.

那間酒店在左邊 / 右邊。

He <u>turned his back on</u> us.

他轉身背對着我們。

He had been hit <u>on the head</u>.

他被打中了腦袋。

There are trees on both sides of the road.

街道兩旁都種了樹。

They live on the first floor.

他們住在二樓。

She lives on Hong Kong Island / Lantau Island.

她住在香港島 / 大嶼山。

Try to remember

There are too many books on my desk.

我桌上有太多書。

Ow! You are standing on my foot.

哎呀！你踩到我的腳。

Other examples

I think your suitcase is on the top of the cupboard.

我想你的手提箱在衣櫃頂上。

Our house is the first one on the left after the police station.

我們的房子是過了警局後靠左第一幢。

Try the test

☐　1. He accepted the cup on behalf of the team.

☐　2. He accepted the cup in behalf of the team.

1. ✓　2. ✗

190 表示 "關於、涉及" 用 on

on 用作介詞時，也是 "關於、涉及" 的意思。例如：

Did you see that documentary on volcanoes last night?

你昨晚有沒有看關於光的紀錄片？

There will be a debate on financial crisis tomorrow.

明天將有一場關於金融危機的辯論。

The Chief Executive refused to comment on the allegations.

行政總裁不肯評論這些指控。

Criticism has no effect on him.

批評影響不了他。

Have the police got anything on you?

警察有沒有抓住你的把柄？

My new bicycle has nothing / does not have anything on the one
that was stolen.

我的新自行車遠遠不及被偷的那輛好。

Try to remember

The pressure on him was enormous.

他承受很大壓力。

Police opened fire on a mob.

警察向暴民開火。

Other examples

I had no formal qualifications when I started working here so I
was given on-the-job training.

我在這裏剛開始工作時沒有正式資格。

You blame it on each other.

你們互相把這事歸咎對方。

以下是含 on 的口語：

have a lot on	很忙
(just) not on	不允許
What's he / she on?	他 / 她在搞甚麼鬼？
What's he / she on about?	他 / 她在說甚麼？

Try the test

☐　1.　The nurse is in call for emergency cases.

☐　2.　The nurse is on call for emergency cases.

1. ✗　　2. ✓

Postscript
後 記

　　在寫書的過程裏，我常常問自己讀者會否喜歡看我的書。目前很多讀者已對英語學習採取放棄態度，尤其是香港的中學在政府的語文和教育政策影響下，那些在中文中學或第二三組別學校讀書的學生，大多對英語學習已失去信心或完全沒有興趣。他們初中時英語水平可能已很差，到了中學畢業仍然同樣差劣，對他們將來進修或謀生造成很大限制。

　　另一方面，自從回歸以來，社會上不少人主張兩文三語，一夜之間中文的地位大大提高，英語的重要性下降，間接造成很多人不再那麼看重英語。但經過十七年後，中英文水平變成怎樣呢？這裏我要引用十多年前香港教育學院語文教育學院院長陳永明教授在接受訪問時所說的幾句話。他說："香港學生的語文水平日漸低落是不爭的事實……中文水平下降的速度比英文更快，情況更嚴重"。

　　也許有人說，我們母語是中文，即使中文水平下降，語言溝通能力是沒問題的。由於我不是中文老師，對於這一觀點我無法判斷是否正確。但目前我看到的事實是，要學生寫報告 / 會議紀錄、投訴信 / 應徵信、建議書或公佈 / 通告等，他們一定覺得用英文寫比較容易，並且很快完成。我鼓勵大家學好英語，是因為英語是有效的溝通工具。

　　最後，作為一個英語老師，我強調學好英語，只是因為英語是國際語言，也是最新科技和知識的傳播媒介。當然，在這方面，一定有人說現時的機器和電腦翻譯不是很方便嗎？沒錯，機器和電腦翻譯的效率非常高，但相信大家一定知道，除了詞彙翻譯得準確之外，它們其他的翻譯實在是茶餘飯後的笑話。例如："咬我"（Bite me）、"你吸"（You suck）、"給我五"（Give me five）、"讓自己在家裏"（Make yourself at home）、"幫助你們"甚至"救救自己"（Help yourself）等，實在不忍卒睹。你真認為用它們翻譯的文章可靠嗎？

　　筆者從事翻譯和語文教學工作，素來強調文章必須通達。與翻譯比較，英語學習實在簡單得多。大家只要努力學好英語各個主要範疇，自然可以提高英語水平。日後如有任何英語上的問題，可以寫電郵給我 culchoi@yahoo.com.hk。